CW01666485

PANTHER JOHN

Robert Tralins

NEW ENGLISH LIBRARY/TIMES MIRROR

First published in the USA in 1970 by Lancer Books, Inc

© 1970 by Robert Tralins

First NEL Paperback Edition May 1980

Conditions of sale: This book is sold subject to the condition that it shall not, by way of trade or otherwise, be lent, resold, hired out, or otherwise circulated without the publisher's prior consent in any form of binding or cover other than that in which it is published and without a similar condition including this condition being imposed on the subsequent purchaser.

NEL Books are published by
New English Library Limited from
Barnard's Inn, Holborn,
London EC1N 2JR.
Made and printed in Great Britain by
Hunt Barnard Printing Ltd.,
Aylesbury, Bucks.

45004782 2

GASPARILLA ISLAND, FLORIDA,
TERRITORY OF SPAIN
March 12, 1811
Friday

Twilight rolled across the sky like a gigantic sail of blue-black canvas, its billowing folds unfurling to blot out the light of day and leave myriads of timid stars in its place gleaming like clusters of gem stones on a celestial carpet of velvet. Gradually the stars began to brighten into tiaras of sparkling constellations that grew more brilliant with each passing moment while the final rosy tint staining the heavens faded as the sun retreated. Faintly, the lapping of the Gulf waters spilling gently upon the flat sand of the beach could be heard sloughing above the tranquil drone of insects and the occasional chirping of sea birds. Then, approaching from the south there came the sound of voices, the laughter of a girl, her tone muted, the solemn baritone of a man, his voice speaking softly, guarded. As the couple approached the deserted beach, fiddler crabs and sand fleas skittered out of their way, seeking protection from the intruders within secret tunnels and hiding places along the strand.

The couple, a tall young Negro of twenty and a nutmeg-complexioned woolly-headed girl of sixteen, paused at the water's edge and embraced. Behind them, from the opposite shore of the narrow, half-mile-wide island, the campfires of Leon and Don Jose Gaspar's pirate crews illuminated the tall palms, glowing above Gasparilla Sound like a stain of blood upon a night-black pennant emblazoned with skull and crossbones.

From the direction of the pirate camp from which they had just stealthily managed to depart without being seen, the couple heard the screams of hilarity and off-key voices of the crews raised in drunken carousal and song as their wax-lights and torches and cookfires illuminated the outdoor mess hall with pulsing gushers of light. Now and again could be heard the clink of a chain as the slaves, most of them hobbled and manacled, cleared away the crude tables and stole discarded or disgorged scraps of meat, some of which they devoured in furtive gulps, but most of which they managed to sneak back to their outdoor pens to share with the less fortunate of their fellows who numbered on that day, some 166 souls.

In the center of the Gaspar brothers' camp was a clearing around which a cluster of crude shelters had been constructed. On the bluff overlooking Gasparilla Inlet where the two ships belonging to the Gaspars were moored in the channel was the log stockade, a fortress-like building in which the pirate captains lived whenever they were ashore. At the far western-most edge of the clearing was a raised platform upon which the padre, on certain rare occasions, blessed the company. The platform was now occupied by four bearded seamen, one with guitar, one with flute, one with fiddle, and the latter with a bull-roarer. The minstrels were leading the crews in song while two plump white women, bared breasts swinging free like white melons of flesh, made their ways among the men pouring grog from heavy earthenware pitchers. The women passed laughing and giggling, pausing only to tweak a nose or tug at a beard or to pour forth rum into mugs and tankards and cups. They did not appear to mind being pawed by groping hands that pinched their buttocks and cupped or twitted their breasts. The scene was a bedlam of boisterous rampant hilarity, punctuated now and then with shrieks of pain, screams, curses, an occasional pistol shot or clanging ring of a steel blade. On the easternmost edge of the clearing a reeling gang of bare-chested seamen was having sport with a naked Negro wench of fourteen whom they were forcing to walk blindfolded across a narrow board which had been placed on crosstrees so it was several feet above the glowing coals of a charcoal fire. On the northside of the encampment, beneath a thatched roof shed, eight men lay upon pallets, naked, oblivious to the others present as nude slave women did their best to pleasure them. The women, ranging in color from jet black to tawny mulatto, were aged fourteen to twenty years and were from the concubinage cribs where they and their sisters were fed, housed, and kept penned in solely for the pleasure of the Gaspar brothers' crews.

During the early stages of the uproar which had begun

shortly before sundown that day, as so many other orgies of drunkenness and debauchery had also taken place during the years the Gaspars and their men had bivouacked on the island they had named for themselves, Juan, the muscular young black man who had been Leon Gaspar's slave, cabin boy, and body servant for a decade, ever since he had been dragged from his slave mother's arms at the age of ten, stole into Gaspar's private quarters in the longhouse and unbolted the door to the chamber beyond in which the sixteen-year-old pearl of Africa, Maha, was imprisoned. When they were sure they would be able to escape undetected, he led Maha out of the luxuriously furnished prison and they crept away from the encampment.

As soon as they were out of sight of the camp and in the jungle they began to run, hand in hand, toward the beach on the Gulf shore. They did not speak until they had stopped running and knelt in the sand at the water's edge, laughing, breathless, and elated.

The girl, smiling demurely up at him reached her hands toward his shoulders and gently dug her fingers under the broadcloth of his shirt. 'You're still sure you want to go through with this?' she asked, her voice an octave above a whisper.

'I know what I'm doing, Maha,' he said. 'Yes, this is what I want. I'm more certain than ever.'

Her fingers tightened on his flesh and she rose up on her knees to kiss him. He returned her kiss and got up, pulling her by the hand. 'We'd better keep to the fringes of the jungle until we've skirted the island. The lookouts might still be sober.'

The girl nodded and followed. Several minutes later, when they arrived at the northernmost tip of the island, the girl laughed with relief. She paused at the water's edge and drew him to her. Then she curled her arms around his neck and stood on tiptoes to kiss him. They embraced for a long moment, then when he disengaged her arms he tugged her by the hand and began to run, laughing quietly down at her as she raced breathlessly trying to keep apace with his long-legged stride. When they reached the bluff which overlooked the inlet where the two vessels were moored in the basin between themselves and the pirate camp at the other shore, they moved into the trees and walked cautiously, taking care to keep in the shadows. When they reached the crude pier where the longboats and the gig in which the crews used to go out to the ships were moored, they crouched and remained in hiding behind a hogshead, waiting until a rising flood of light from the moon was blotted from view by a passing cloud.

Suddenly, from behind a barrel on the crude pier beyond, a shadowy figure, like a tall spectre without a face, arose and beckoned to them.

The girl's fingers tightened in Juan's hand, her nails digging into his calloused palm. She gasped in fright and moved against him, looking up into his eyes with alarm.

'It's Gideon,' Juan explained. 'He and Boko and several of the other slaves who can be trusted are making the break with us.'

'But you didn't tell me there would be others – won't that be too dangerous?'

Juan laughed. 'Not at all. We'll need a crew and all the help we can get.'

'What for? To get away in that little gig? I could sail that myself.'

Juan nodded. 'We're not taking the gig. We'd never get away in that. Instead we're taking the *Mer Jewel*.'

'Leon Gaspar's flagship?' she cried, forgetting herself for a moment, then clapping a hand to her mouth as though to stifle her own outcry. 'But – you can't – that's insane. You're only a black man and a slave . . . '

At her words Juan stiffened. He looked into her upturned face. 'And I suppose you're a goddamn white woman and a free one *at that*?'

'No, I didn't mean it like that,' she said, biting her lip and glancing toward the beckoning figure in apprehension. 'I meant that it's just crazy.'

'Why?'

She averted her gaze and shrugged.

'Don't you want to get away from here? All those things you told me these past two months Gaspar's kept you locked in his strongroom – did you mean them – about being in love with me – and all the rest?'

The girl raised her head. Tears were glistening in her eyes as she whispered, 'Yes, oh, but I do mean it, Juan. I do love you. But just the same, this is insanity.'

'It's no more insane than what I'm doing now – Gaspar's

body servant cheating him out of deflowering his prize wench and running off with her to boot.'

'I'm *not* his wench!'

'This is hardly the time to vent your pride – your royal highness.'

'Please, Juan, don't be cynical. I apologize. Perhaps you can't understand how it has been with me. You've been a pirate for too long to be able to – '

'That has nothing to do with my cynicism. Like yourself, I'm one of those fortunate black people who has the advantage of an education.'

'I know,' she said, hanging her head in humility. 'I only want you to know I'm not accustomed to this sort of thing. My father, the king of the Coromantees, did not prepare me for such a fate. Being Gaspar's prisoner – and slave – these past months ever since he bought me from those dreadful Arab slavers has done something to me. It's been like a nightmare you can't escape until you wake up.' Her voice mellowed and she gazed raptly at him, her hand touching his forearm. 'But thank God for you, I've been roused and awakened and I've escaped the nightmare. Had it not been for you, Juan, God only knows what I would have done.' Her fingers caressed his flesh devotedly. 'Can you understand what I've been through? Can you possibly know what it is to be a princess at a missionary school one minute and then be in chains the next?' She broke off for a moment and then knelt back on her haunches to smile at him. 'Dearest Juan,' she whispered, her voice tremulous with feeling, 'I love you – truly I do. If Gaspar were to catch us and put us to death I would not feel cheated for at least I've had these precious moments with you . . . '

'Don't talk like that, Maha. I've planned this carefully down to the last detail. Neither Leon nor Don Jose Gaspar will catch us. You'll see, we'll be free before the sun rises again. Come now, we've talked enough and tarried for too long. The clouds are over the moon.' He stood and pulled her up by the hand. Then they ran along the hand-hewn timbers of the pier toward the waiting Gideon.

'All is in readiness, sar,' Gideon said when they reached his side. 'Boko and the others are awaiting us aboard the *Mer Jewel*. I have scuttled the longboat and Michel is at this moment about to put the torch to Don Jose's vessel.'

'Michel!' Juan hissed. '*He* can't be trusted.'

'There was no one else I cared to send.'
'Why?'
'Boko is needed for navigation and the others are all experienced seamen. Only Michel knows how to swim. Only he knows nothing of seamanship. Therefore, I sent him.'
'And if he betrays us?'
Gideon grinned, the white teeth in his shadowy face gleaming. 'If he does, we have lost nothing. The crews of the Gaspars will not be able to go out to the corvette in time to overtake us. The sloop is by far the swifter of the two vessels, is it not?'
Juan smiled and nodded. 'Very well, Gideon. Shall we be off?'
Gideon looked around them for several moments, then he arose, beckoning. Juan and Maha followed him to the end of the pier. They descended to the gig. Gideon took up the oars as Juan cast off the mooring lines. As they rowed by the other small boats Juan saw with a glance that Gideon had done his job well, for the oars were floating out into the sound with the flooding tide and each boat was slowly sinking.
Before them loomed the two pirate ships. The sloop, a twenty-gun French-built brigantine rigged vessel had been Leon Gaspar's pride and joy. It amused Juan to think that he was not only about to steal it, but that he was as well taking his master's prize virgin wench also. As they drew near the two vessels and passed beneath the mooring lines which spanned the inlet to palm trees ashore, Juan stood in the prow of the gig and peered at the barkentine beyond. After several minutes he turned, frowning, and looked at Gideon. 'How long has Michel been aboard?'
Gideon paused, resting his oars on the gunwales. He turned to glance toward the ship. 'At sundown he went over the side, sar. I saw him myself swimming toward her.'
'He should have cleaved a tidy hole in her bottom by now.'
'No, sar,' Gideon said. 'I told him to put the torch to her as soon as he saw us unfurl the sails. I thought better of having him chop through her bottom. You know how the sound of an axe carries across the water on still nights like this.'
Juan nodded. He looked toward Maha and smiled. 'You see, we need Gideon. His wisdom is great.'

Maha smiled and nodded. She studied the face of the powerful Negro and marveled at the ease with which he pulled the oars which sent them moving swiftly toward the hull which was now looming three stories above them. When they came alongside several of the slaves aboard waved excitedly and dropped lines to them. Gideon unshipped the oars and as he made the lines secure to the rings fore and aft so the gig could be hoisted aboard, Juan caught the rungs of a rope ladder and helped Maha climb up. She went up without hesitation, eager and anxious.

The moment Juan climbed over the bulwarks after she had been helped to the deck, the other slaves crowded round to embrace him and express their gratitude and excitement. With a low laugh Juan chastised them, 'What are you standing here for? Let's get on with it, my hearties. Get aloft with the lot of you and let's put to sea.'

As the eleven slaves scampered up the masts and stays and blended with the shadows in the rigging, Boko came forward from the quarterdeck with a brace of pistols and a cutlass which he had taken from Gaspar's arms locker in the pirate's main cabin. He said nothing as he held the weapons out to Juan. The gesture clearly showed the warm feeling he had for the young Negro he and the others had unanimously appointed their captain. Juan took the pistols and held them up in the light of the moon. The others, aloft, paused in their work of unfurling the sheets to watch. Then Juan placed the pistols in his waistband and took the cutlass. He turned several times, slashing it in the air. Gideon climbed the ladder to the quarterdeck and stood grinning, tears of joy unabashedly streaming down his face. Gideon had spent thirty of his forty years in captivity. When Juan Gomez had been taken aboard, it had been Gideon who had taught the ten-year-old boy how to serve his master. Later, as the years elapsed, it had been Gideon who had taught Juan how to read, cipher and write, how to navigate a vessel and how to use cutlass, pistol and cannon. Gideon indeed was the one man aboard who was singularly responsible for bringing about this coup – it was a day he had dreamed of for most of his life – a day when he would escape from Gaspar and his pirate crew forever. He had read this in the ashes which Boko, the voodoo *hungan* had sprinkled on the palms of his hands one day many years before. The *hungan* had told him in the Creole *patois*, 'Gideon, the day will come when one young man you will love like a son will rise up and take you to freedom. This young man will do all that your master can do and he will do it better. This is my prophecy.'

For that day, Gideon had lived, and now that it had finally arrived, he was overwhelmed with joy. He had no fears or misgivings. He was utterly confident in the success of their endeavor and as he stood to one side watching Juan assume command of the ship they had sneaked aboard, he was choked with emotion.

Juan turned and smiled at Gideon. He handed him the cutlass Boko had given him and said, 'Gideon, I will never forget all you have taught me. You shall see, I will lead you and the others to glory and freedom!'

Gideon bowed in humility. 'My capitaine, sar. I will follow you to the death. I will be your right arm.' He then lifted the blade aloft and stepped forward to embrace Juan.

The others in the rigging watched in silence. They too saluted Juan.

After several long moments Juan stepped back and gave Gideon a playful punch in the chest. 'Let's cast off, first officer.'

'Aye!' Gideon cried, whirling and moving to the aft mooring lines. He struck the blade down across the hawser, severing it, and at once the vessel gave a lurch as the tide began to carry it toward the narrow channel leading into the sound and the Gulf of Mexico beyond.

Suddenly, as the craft began to turn there was a cry of alarm from one of the slaves in the rigging aloft. In the dim light Juan saw Leon Gaspar standing on the weather rail, cutlass in hand as two other men climbed over to join him.

'So, nigger!' Gaspar shouted, 'this is how you repay your master for treating you like a white man! I'll show you that a black man can't steal from his master.' With that, Gaspar jumped down and began to charge at Juan.

Gideon stepped forward but Juan yelled for him to stop. 'Your blade, Gideon,' he said, swiftly moving to Gideon's side.

The tall Negro tossed the cutlass toward Juan. Juan caught it and expertly parried Gaspar's first thrust. Then the tall young man jumped up lightly to the narrow rail forward of the quarterdeck and struck expertly to parry another savage thrust from the pirate captain's blade. He laughed and jumped down to the deck again and lightly danced out of range each time Gaspar waded toward him, wildly slashing with his blade. In the moonlight the pirate's red silk blouse and bright yellow headscarf was a blur of color as he again and again lunged at Juan, but each time the agile young black man laughed and sidestepped.

One of the men who had boarded the ship with Gaspar brought up a pistol. Before he could take aim, Boko threw a knife. The blade thudded into his chest and the man fell backward over the rail, screaming, the pistol discharging harmlessly in the air. The second man cursed and rushed toward Boko but before he could take two steps one of the men in the rigging dove down at him. He brought the pirate to the deck and dispatched him with a sheath knife.

'Kill Gaspar, Juan!' cried several of the men from aloft.

Juan laughed and stepped in easily just as Gaspar tried to decapitate him with an arcing swing of the blade. He drove his cutlass down against Gaspar's blade hilt and twisted. The pirate captain's weapon went flying out of his hand.

Juan then stepped in and held his blade against Gaspar's throat. 'Beg for your life, white master,' Juan said. 'Beg!'

Gaspar dropped to his knees, for a moment beseeching Juan with his eyes, then lifting his hands he whispered, 'Quarter!'

'Kiss my boots and beg for your life!'

Gaspar at once bent his lips to Juan's boots. Then he sat up on his knees and silently glowered. 'I beg ye spare me, Juan.'

'Panther John,' Juan said. 'Call me Panther John.'

'Aye, Panther John. I beg ye to spare me.'

Juan smiled and stepped back, lowering his blade. He then turned to Gideon and said, 'He has done more to you than any other man with us. Would you like the honor of throwing him overboard?'

Gideon's eyes gleamed as he nodded and stepped forward. He had waited a lifetime for that moment. He seized Gaspar by the scruff of the neck and the back of his belt and lifted him over his head. Holding the stocky two-hundred-pound man high in the air, Gideon's powerful muscles bulged as he walked to the gunwales and then heaved him over the side.

At the sound of the splash made when Gaspar's body hit the water, a rousing cheer went up from the men. Juan turned and saw Maha coming toward him, climbing up the quarterdeck ladder. She was beaming with joy as she said,

'Juan, you've done it – you've really done it!'

He nodded and glanced up at the unfurling sails, noting with satisfaction how they began to billow out in the breeze. Then he placed the cutlass through his belt and held a hand out to her. She came toward him, smiling up into his face. 'Why didn't you kill him when you had the chance? If it had been the other way around he certainly would've killed you.'

Juan did not smile as he looked down at her. 'To have killed him would have made me no better than he is. But to have spared him, that proves *I* am the master now.'

OFF THE COAST OF FLORIDA,
THE GULF OF MEXICO
March 14, 1811
Sunday
7 a.m.

Juan stood beside the helmsman, silently scanning the islands at the southwestern end of Florida through the spyglass he had found in Leon Gaspar's sea chest. Although the lookouts aloft in the crow's nest had not sighted a sail since they had commanded the *Mer Jewel* and fled from Gasparilla Island, Juan and the men knew it would not be long before the brothers Gaspar and perhaps too, the entire pirate brotherhood would be pursuing them. Because the vessel had not been provisioned with ample food and water prior to its capture, the primary concern of the crew was to locate a hidden island where they might make their headquarters until deciding what to do.

Several months before Gasper had brought Maha to the island stronghold, Gideon and Juan had discussed what they might do when and if the opportunity ever arose for them to steal one of the pirate ships and escape. Although Juan believed at that time it was a mere futile dream which would never become reality, he was amused now when he thought of it, that it had taken a female to make him *want* to make that dream come true. As he stood in the bright morning sunshine of freedom resplendent in the pantaloons and bright yellow shirt and captain's hat that had been Gaspar's, he felt as though he had been reborn and though he had some trepidation, he knew now, for the first time in his life, that he would sooner die than return to slavery.

During Gideon's long talks with him over the years, Juan had allowed himself the luxury of dreaming of the day when they might be really free; free to do as they wished; free to go anywhere in the world they wished – as free men and not slaves. But this had only been a dream. Even though he and Gideon were able to read and write in

English, Spanish and in French, and though they had a speaking knowledge of Portuguese, somehow they never quite equated themselves with the white men who were their masters. Both men had been born and bred into slavery and had not known any other way of life; but now, now that they were on their own, and now that they knew they were in danger of being recaptured, suddenly they began to taste the feeling of responsibility that comes with freedom and they agreed it was worth fighting – and possibly, dying for.

From the moment when he decided to make his move, Juan had told Gideon, and later, Boko, that he had been motivated into making his move because he was in love with Maha and wanted her more than he wanted to live: from that moment on he had become a different man. Both Gideon and Boko smiled at this confession. Both men had lived for the day when the youthful Panther John would come to his senses and lead them away from bondage. Both men had always known that Juan Gomez, the young man with the physique of a Goliath and the grace of a black panther would one day best the great Leon Gaspar – and he had done so, but Juan had disappointed them by not slaying the white pirate. Neither Gideon nor Boko would admit aloud the fear that one day Juan would live to regret having spared Gaspar's life; nevertheless, they were grateful. For many years during Juan's servitude to Gaspar he had soaked up everything there was to learn about ships and sailing and navigation and gunnery and hand-to-hand combat. For many years he had secretly learned the arts and wiles of captaining a pirate crew and though he had kept silent, with his ears and eyes always alert to learn something new, never once did Leon or his brother, Don Jose Gaspar, ever suspect that the quiet-spoken subservient black man whom they called jokingly, Panther John, would one day rise up against them. Only the Negro slaves knew that Panther John, despite his youth, was destined to become a great and bold man – a man who would lead them and other men. They had come to know this because they had observed him while they suffered in silence without daring to complain. They had come to know this because he was the symbol of all they hoped and dreamed for, and through Juan they were able to survive the many cruelties and deprivations the Gaspars inflicted upon them. Collectively, the slaves who had been the Gaspars' ablest seamen were likewise their most subservient slaves, for the years before the mast and flogging post had turned them into obedient zombies without a will. Though superior as seamen in every respect to the free white men who served the freebooter captains, the slaves were never permitted to forget that because of the color of their skins, they were slaves and *not* seamen. Despite this, each man knew – and longed for – that day when one of them would rise up and become their leader, a leader who would lead them out of bondage. Gideon and Boko, and later, other stalwart black seamen in their midst began to look hopefully toward Juan for salvation. Everywhere the young black man went, everything he did, was watched and admired by his fellows, for not only had it been prophesied by the voodoo prophet Boko, but they could see for themselves how Juan was taking to his secret apprenticeship and learning all there was to learn from his master, Leon Gaspar.

Now that the hour had finally come and they were, for the moment, free, they looked to Juan with new hope. Juan felt this spirit through every fibre of his being and he was concerned that he might err, and hence, fail all those who had placed such faith and trust in him.

As he stood that morning scanning the distant islands off the southwestern Florida coast, Juan fixed his mind determinedly on one goal: to remain free. Somewhere along the coast in the myriad of mangroves and islands he knew there was an island where he would take his ship and crew and where they would be able to establish a base for themselves. He knew this because Boko had said there was such a place. He knew he dared not run the risk of staying on the high seas for many weeks until his men were accustomed to freedom and until they had learned to work together like a team. If they were to be confronted by Gaspar and his fighting men before they were prepared, Juan realized his men would fight bravely, but their courage would be no match against experienced, overwhelming numbers of opponents. As slaves the men had been denied the practice or the use of small arms and blade, except for Juan and Gideon, who had been trained to be Gaspar's bodyguards. No one else aboard the vessel had handled a pistol or cutlass before. Although Gideon and Boko were competent gunners, able to place ball or shrapnel accurately, they could not be expected to man the guns without trained gun crews. In short, they were in need of at least twenty additional able-bodied seamen. Even if those aboard knew the nuances of hand-to-hand combat and gunnery or the craft of piracy, they were still undermanned and unable to defend or attack another vessel.

Boko, who had been poring over a chart which had been weighted down on the deck since dawn that morning, suddenly called out to Juan, 'Capitaine, sar! I've found it. Look here, sar!'

Juan knelt on the deck beside him and followed a carefully pencilled course which Boko had just traced on the parchment chart. 'Boko, are you sure? We can't risk running aground – not now.'

'Aye, I'm sure, sar. Though it be many, many y'ar ago, I recall like it was yestiddy. Whilst I was the carpenter mate's boy aboard Calico Jack's frigate we got cotched up with by a two decker with forty guns. A sloop o'war was she, sar. We runned from them fer two days and luck was with us because we runned in them islands and holed up thar. Whilst we was thar waiting them out, Calico hisself sent me out in a dory to find warter. I found warter on this here island. That be the place, sar. I'm rightly sure o'it.' He paused and looked at the starboard quarter of the deck where Gideon was standing with the sextant. 'You got a fix yet, Gid?'

Gideon lowered the instrument and came over. He took the pencil from Boko and on a corner of the chart wrote their position. Then he plotted a course for the channel around the mangrove islands Boko had marked and went to the helm to take over the wheel and set a new course.

Juan and Boko climbed the stays and watched as the bow turned slowly north-northeastward into the morning sun. From where they swung it was possible to see the clear waters of the shore and the smooth sandy bottom below. 'Better send a man forward to take soundings,' Juan said when it became obvious they were in shallow water.

Boko swung down from the line he had been supporting himself upon and ran forward, calling several of the men to follow.

A few minutes later Boko's deep voice made the first call: 'Four-and-a-half fathoms, sar!'

As the vessel proceeded, Gideon ordered the topsails reefed and stood grimly steering the course he had set. All hands came on deck and stood at the bulwarks, watching as the landfall drew nearer. They knew what would happen if they ran aground.

No one spoke a word during the two hours it took to find the channel. As they slowly wound their way past the jagged mangrove islands along the southern coast of Florida, Juan stood on the bowsprit, giving directional hand-signals to Gideon on the quarterdeck aft. When the call, 'One fathom, sar!' rang out, Gideon shouted an order for all hands aloft to lower the main peak and haul the helm up. He wanted to be ready to pull free the moment the bottom was felt bumping upon the shoals.

Maha, who had come forward to stand apprehensively biting her fingers as she watched Juan give hand-signals to Gideon, was the first to notice they had entered a blue water passage that arced northward through a natural coral channel between two small islands. Pointing, Maha cried out in excitement. The moment the crew saw what she was shouting about, they joined her in a rousing cheer.

'Thar she be, sar!' cried Boko, climbing the shrouds to get a better view of the larger island to starboard. He doffed his cap and waving it, cried, 'We now has got ourselves a better hideaway than the Gaspars got. I hereby dubs yon island in honor o'our fine capitaine, Juan Gomez.'

'No, no!' Gideon shouted. 'Call it Panther Cay.'

'Hear, hear!' nodded several of the men.

'So be it!' Boko laughed, looking down at Juan for approval.

Juan smiled at him, then looked at Maha. She was elated and her face shone in the sunlight.

'Yonder point,' Boko shouted again, 'I hereby dub Gomez Point, in honor of our capitaine.'

'Hear, hear!' the men shouted and applauded.

Juan stepped lightly down to the deck from the bowsprit just as the men went berserk with joy. They lifted Juan bodily to their shoulders and began to carry him amidships, shouting and laughing like frolicking children who had just won an athletic contest against a team of bullies. Juan reached up and caught a handhold on the starboard ratlines. He swung himself up and stood, one foot and one hand on the lines, several feet above their heads, laughing down at them and trying to silence them with gestures. When they finally fell silent, Juan told them: 'My hearties, let's not celebrate before there's something to celebrate. Now that we've found this here island what Boko told us about, there's work to be done. Before we go ashore I want it understood from this moment on we must all stand together like brothers.'

'That we will do!' cried one of the older men, a short man with brown weathered skin who was called Tubal.

Juan smiled at him. 'Tubal, you and Nimrod will see that the water barrels are filled.' He waited until the man nodded, then he addressed his next remark to an old man whose blue-black complexion bespoke of the years he had spent before the mast under tropical suns. 'Joab, you will take the first watch aloft. Keep a sharp lookout, my hearty.'

'Aye!' Joab said, touching one hand to his scarf-covered head by way of saluting, and then promptly leaping up, caught the shrouds and went up with the agility and speed of a simian who had spent its life in the trees.

'The rest of you,' Juan said, 'will divide into two companies. One will come under Gideon's command, the other, under Boko's. That way the work will be divided equally and we'll accomplish much more than if we don't organize ourselves.'

Nods of approval were seen as the men dispersed. At the helm, Gideon gave the commands that sent them aloft to furl the sails, while Boko took charge of the gang forward and aft whose duty it was to play out the mooring lines and anchor cables once the hooks were let fall.

Maha stood beside Juan, her head resting on his shoulder as they watched the men bring the vessel to a halt a few yards from a stand of palmetto palms ashore. The gangway was lowered and two men went ashore and caught the lines which they secured to the gnarled roots of several large mangrove trees. When the vessel was secured, the men mustered on deck awaiting orders from Juan. Gideon and Boko huddled with Juan and it was decided that half the men would go on a hunting party while the others would remain with Boko to construct shelters on a high point of land about five hundred yards from where they were moored. Once their camp was established two cannons would be placed in a fortification to guard the channel entrance leading to the anchorage.

Later that afternoon, when the men were occupied with their duties, Juan and Maha boarded the gig and sailed around the island to make certain there were no other passages through which a vessel might approach their camp.

As the couple sat in the craft, lazily sailing the waters on the east shore, small sail billowing in the light breeze, flocks of flamingo and wild duck were seen flying overhead. Here and there fish leaped from the sparkling clear water, and along the muddy banks of mangrove could be seen exotic birds, spoonbills and herons as they idly searched for food. 'This part of the country reminds me of Africa,' Maha said, sitting closer to Juan, nestling her head upon his chest. 'Juan, do you think I'll ever see my home again?'

'Perhaps some day,' he said absently.

'Will you take me, if you can?'

He thought a moment and replied, 'If I can, and if – '

'If, *what*?'

'If we can sail the *Mer Jewel* across the Atlantic sea. It's a big sea, you know.'

'I know. It took us nearly a month to cross when they brought me in the slave ship.'

'Sometimes it takes longer and the voyage can be dangerous on account of the storms – and other perils.'

'Such as?'

'Pirates. Pirate hunters. Becalmed waters. The Sargasso Sea . . . '

'What's that?' she asked, sitting forward, turning her face to peer up at him.

'A vast becalmed sea of strange weeds. It is said that when a ship ventures into it there is no escape.'

'You would not venture into it,' she said. 'And if you did, I'm sure you would find a way to escape.' She smiled and put her arms around his neck. Her lips drew close to his and she licked his upper lip, then hungrily drove her mouth against his. Juan's arms went around her. Untended, the tiller of the small gig turned and the vessel began to drift aimlessly as the slack sails fluttered and flapped as though in applause of being untended.

'Maha, my princess,' Jaun said in a whisper, 'if taking you back to your people means losing you, I don't want that. I want you with me always. You are all things to me. With you, my life has purpose and meaning. Before I knew you, before you were brought to Gasparilla, I lived from day to day without caring or thinking of the future, though Gideon and the others always said it was ordained that I should lead them to freedom. Perhaps it was fate that brought you to me, and made me make the prophecy come true.'

'Perhaps,' she said, kissing him again.

'Because of you my life and the lives of all those who fled with us have been changed. This frightens me.'

'You, *afraid*? I cannot believe that, Juan.'

'Yes, it's true. Everyone is afraid, even the bravest, even Gaspar. But my fear is a little different. I fear the future, the responsibility I have for the lives of all those who depend on me now. I fear for your comfort and safety, and I fear that I am asking you to give up your life by asking you to stay with me. The future promises to be a constant fight to stay free. I know Leon Gaspar as I know no other man. I know he will hunt me down if it takes the rest of his life. Our life together may not be as blissful as you might believe. The woman of a runaway slave, a brigand, is not destined to be like other women. We cannot stay here forever. The men will soon be restless. They will want women, and other things. When Boko spoke to me of the future he reminded me that I will not be master of my fate, but that fate will be my master. Just as my crew will be loyal to me, I must be likewise loyal to them, even if it means sacrificing my own happiness. Can you understand that?'

Maha nodded. 'You forget, I am the daughter of a Coromantee king. I learned at an early age that one who is born to rule is a slave to his people. I also learned that it is unwise to worry about or fear the future. Our witch doctors were wise, just as I'm certain Boko, your prophet, is wise, but nevertheless, when my father sent me to the Christian school where I was educated and where I learned the white man's languages, I also learned I would rather live my own life, even if it is for only a few days or months, than I would live someone else's. What I mean is I don't care if Boko's prophecy is true or if it will come true. My fate is in your hands, in your arms, and I intend to be your woman no matter what, even if I should die tonight, for to have been yours, even for a little while, would be worth it. So what you say about spending the rest of your life running from Gaspar, or hiding from him, matters little to me. Of course I would rather that you and I could go some place far away where he couldn't find us, but I know that cannot be either. You were ordained to be free and the only freedom you can possibly have as a black man is the freedom you have chosen.'

'What are you trying to say, Maha?'

She eyed him and smiled. After a long pause she sighed and said, 'Simply that you've been with the pirates since boyhood and it's the only life you know. When you and your men will have settled down, you will want to take the *Mer Jewel* to sea – and you will follow your instincts – to whatever will be.'

'Whatever will be?' he asked, smiling a little.

Nodding, she laughed. 'You are a born pirate captain, a leader of men. The ship is your dominion, the crew, your people. You will practice the craft of piracy because you will have no other choice . . . '

'For so young and beautiful a girl, you astonish me.'

'Why should that astonish you, Juan? It is as obvious to me as the mosquitoes that buzz around us this minute. I know you my dear, and I love you. I don't want to change you, I want you to be as you are, for that is the only way I can be happy. I love you for who you are and one does not try to change the nature of a loved one. Therefore, I am content.' She laughed, then added, 'Come, my beautiful man, make love to me. Give me your strength, your arms.'

Juan slid down to the bottom of the boat, taking her into his arms, drawing her against him gently. His hands stroked her as his lips sought her. She moved easily on top of him as they reclined, he on the bottom upon his back, she on top of him, prone, her body sensuous against his muscular one. He began to unbutton the fastenings of the silk dress she was wearing, the one he had given her – the one that he had found in Gaspar's sea chest – the garment among many others which the pirate had taken from his victims at sea.

When she was naked against his naked body, Maha's mouth leeched upon the flesh of his shoulder as her slim legs clasped his narrow hips. Her body, sleek and supple in the delicious warmth of the sun electrified him with desire. He did not wish merely to possess Maha as he had so often possessed other women, he wanted to love her, to become part of her, and to take part of her into himself. The throbbing sensation of her eager womanhood encompassing his rigid member in one impatient gulp brought forth from his lips a groan of ecstasy. He clenched his teeth and clawed her buttocks against him, digging deep his powerful fingers. He felt her sharp teeth biting his shoulder, then his chest, then his earlobes, and he responded by contorting himself to place his mouth upon her breast, the small rounded bowl of brown tinted flesh and its pinkish tip, the flesh he wanted so to sink his teeth into, but dared not for fear of hurting her. He had no wish to hurt this woman, this child-woman whom he loved so desperately. He wanted her to bear his children, to be at his side for the rest of his days; and as he instinctively felt himself plunging into her the urge to impregnate her came over him; it was a sensation he had never before known and it was encompassing, engulfing, all-powerful and overwhelming. The savagery of their lovemaking dissolved to tenderness at the culmination of it all, and the tenderness dissolved to weeping as mouths together, tasting of salt and tears, tongues mingling, communicated and communicating, they clung to each other as though it was the only way to hold onto life one moment longer . . . one sublime moment longer.

Later, as they languished in the sun, the warmth of the sunlight dried the moisture from their flesh like dewdrops evaporating from the petals of wild flowers growing free in the wilderness and they realized for the first time they were free – and really not free.

PANTHER CAY
March 31, 1811
Wednesday
8 a.m.

Juan stared blankly out the window of his quarters at the serene waters of the Gulf of Mexico, watching the shimmering surface as prisms of mirrored sunlight reflected like flashing gems upon the palms and sands along the southern fringes of the island. During the first few days on the island, Juan and his men had built rough log shelters for themselves which they fashioned from the tropical trees growing on the island. They covered the roofs with thatched palm fronds and built tables and chairs and beds from rough hewn timbers. On the highest point of the island they erected a fortification in which two carronade from the ship were installed on wooden tracks so they could be aimed in any direction of the compass or raised to any elevation at will in order to guard the seaward approaches. There was no way of knowing when – or if – the Gaspar brothers' ships would venture near in search of them and Juan did not wish to confront them unprepared.

A week before, Gideon and Boko had left the island for the city of Key West at Thompson's Island where they hoped to find and recruit more experienced seamen which they so desperately needed to man the ship. They sailed away in the longboat, taking along ample provisions and a small pouch containing a quantity of gold coins. But now that a week had elapsed and they were already two days overdue, Juan was becoming restless and impatient. The two men had promised to return by Monday afternoon with twenty new hands. Now it was Wednesday. Juan fretted about this, wondering if something had happened.

From the crude bed in the room behind him, Maha stirred and opened her eyes. For a long while she watched him, knowing how he was worrying about Gideon and Boko. She knew she dared not say anything to him in his present frame of mind for it was not a woman's place to do so unless she was first asked to speak. From the slight sag of his broad shoulders and the manner in which he slumped against the logs of the wall, Maha knew he was in a dejected mood. She did not like to see him like that, solemn and occupied with his thoughts, unsmiling, and grim-jawed, and she knew she could only try to cheer him by taking his mind from his troubles. In a way, she secretly hoped Gideon and Boko would be unsuccessful in their efforts to recruit new men, for she did not want Juan to go to sea. She knew there would be no stopping him once he got a crew together and went to sea on a course of piracy. Although he had not told her in so many words of his intentions, she knew he intended to become a pirate just as soon as he had ample men to man his ship. There was a quality of untapped ambition within Juan's soul and Maha had been the first to recognize it, despite the fact that Boko and Gideon both had always believed it to be there too. Deep inside him was a burning urge over which he had no conscious control: he was a black man and ex-slave now in a white man's world that one day very shortly he was destined to invade; therefore he was readying himself and his men for that time. He could not do otherwise, for to remain in hiding, in obscurity, was not Juan's way. All this Maha understood. Yet, she was unable to understand *why* she understood these things of Juan or how she came to know them, unless, she rationalized, it was because of her love for him. As she lay abed watching him in brooding silence, tears welled to her eyes. She knew he would make his mark in the world once he was ready to do so; and she also knew Boko's prophecy, that one day Panther John would be the greatest black pirate ever to sail the seven seas, would prove true, no matter if she tried to stop him or not. Had she not seen, on the eve before Gideon's and Boko's departure, how Juan's face was illuminated when Boko sprinkled the ashes and foretold the future, that they would return with twenty stalwart fellows who would make the company into the greatest pirate crew in the world; and further, he continued, with conviction ringing in his rich basso voice, that Panther John, their capitaine would lead them to glory on the high seas she might not have resigned herself to fate. Impassive, Juan had stood in the background, brawny arms folded across his chest, listening in silence. The crew turned and stared in awe at their captain.

At that moment, Gideon removed from beneath his shirt a new flag which he had secretly made. He had wanted to surprise his captain and the crew by showing it when they were all together. Now he moved into the center of the clearing and tied the folded pennant to a makeshift flagstaff. He lifted it into the air and shook it. The pennant unfurled in the breeze. At the sight of it, all hands cheered lustily. Gideon had sewn a golden panther upon the black field of a jolly roger above the white skull and crossbones. The panther had been cut from a piece of gold silk cloth. It was expertly done, perched in a crouch as though ready to spring. Indeed a fitting insignia for the Black Panther and his crew. Gideon turned hopefully, looking to Juan for approval.

Juan smiled. 'The Golden Panther,' he said softly, staring up at the flag. 'I like it.' Then, turning to the men, he asked, 'Gentlemen? Do *you* like it?'

All hands stood up shouting and cheering, applauding Gideon's handiwork with gusto.

'So be it!' Juan cried. 'From this moment forth Gideon's pennant shall be our flag, and the new name of our ship will be the *Golden Panther*! Three cheers for the *Golden Panther* and the man who made the flag!'

When the grog mugs were empty and the cheering had subsided, Juan ordered all mugs filled again. He brought a brimming mug into the center of the clearing and held it aloft. 'Here's to the *Golden Panther* and her crew. May we all live victoriously – and courageously for many years to come.'

That morning as Juan stood staring out at the sea he found himself wondering what he would do if Gideon and Boko failed to return. As he pondered this he felt an emptiness inside as hope deserted him. He knew he depended on the two men, but until that moment had not realized how much. Without them, he doubted if he could alone handle the ship and crew; and he wondered what would happen if they were never heard from again.

At that moment there was the sound of the conch-shell horn from the lookout aloft atop a tall palm tree above the carronade. The men at once began to run toward the fortification, strapping on their belts and shouting excitedly. Juan, naked to the waist, dashed out of the log shelter and raced to the rampart where he looked out at the sea, saw nothing, then called up to the lookout, 'What do you see, matey?'

'Sail ho!' the Negro aloft cried excitedly. ' 'Pears to be Gid and Boko in the longboat – with a gang o'stout fellers.'

Juan called for the spyglass. The lookout tossed it down and Juan caught it. He opened the glass and put it to his eye. At a point due south on the horizon he saw the longboat clearly. From the manner in which her gunwales were riding Juan knew the boat was carrying passengers. Then, as the craft tacked into the wind he saw them. Gideon, astern at the tiller, was chewing a long cigar. Nine figures could be seen on the starboard side and eleven were on the port side. Then Juan recognized Boko. He closed the glass and went over to the lookout's tree. He tied the glass to the lanyard and the lookout pulled the glass back up to his nest again.

A half hour later Gideon, Boko, and the twenty young Negroes they had brought with them disembarked. They were introduced all around and then sat down to breakfast. Over cups of freshly brewed chicory and generous helpings of venison which Tubal and Joab carved from the carcass of a freshly killed key deer which had been roasting on the spit since the evening before, Juan and the others learned that the Negro seamen, all of whom had been slaves aboard a Spanish merchantman, had been freed by Gideon and Boko. The men laughed as they told, in Spanish, the details of how Gideon and Boko had overpowered the ship's watch and then had freed the men. The vessel was moored in the deep water off Thompson's Island at the time.

When Juan addressed the company after they had eaten their fill he told them that from that moment on they would be considered free men and if they swore allegiance to the captain of the *Golden Panther* and the crew, they would share and share alike in all booty. At this the newcomers stood up and applauded, broad smiles upon their faces.

One of the men, a huge Negro with shining bald pate and enormous shoulders, faced Juan and said, 'Señor Panther John, I promise you on behalf o'my comrades that you will not regret this. We will serve you loyally and faithfully. If any man among us fails to do so, you just turn him over to old Piedro – that's me, master.'

'I am not your master,' Juan said. 'I am your captain, not your master. You are no longer slaves. You are free men. *¿Comprende?*'

Two days later the men had settled into a routine that left little time for leisure or caprice. At the crack of dawn each day they breakfasted and then received instructions from Juan, Gideon, and Boko, in the use of small arms and cutlass. Then the entire company boarded the *Golden Panther* and drilled themselves until noon in the routines and procedures of handling the vessel. After lunch and a brief siesta, the men took turns going through the motions of firing, loading, and servicing the guns. Afternoons were employed in the menial labors of scrubbing down the vessel from forepeak to stern until decks, estanchions, gunwales, bulwarks, ladders, brass-works, and quarters from mess to caboose were brilliantly clean. During the early evening hours before the last light of day the men practiced hurling boarding pikes, harpoons, and throwing knives. After supper, around the fires and lanterns, the men sat mending nets, sails, lines, and whetting utensils and knife blades.

Within a week after the crew had been practicing the craft of seamanship under Panther John they began to function like a well drilled naval unit equal to any afloat. But still Juan was not pleased. He wanted his crew to be better than that of any white man's crew and he spared no man from being reminded of this whenever he made his rounds or worked along with Gideon and Boko who were supervising their two divisions. Jaun had spent more than half his life as Leon Gaspar's slave and body servant, and later, as his bodyguard, as had Gideon; therefore he and Gideon knew only too well the many weeks of practice it required before a crew could be considered adequately trained and seaworthy. Unlike the Gaspars, Gideon and Juan both agreed it was far better to train their men together and to treat them kindly than it was to mistreat them and neglect their training. In order to defend themselves at sea against larger ships with more men and guns, they would need to know how to make every maneuver count and how to accomplish more with their fewer numbers. As the days, and then the weeks passed, the crew of the *Golden Panther* rapidly began to work as a precision team and as their efficiency increased it became more evident they could outperform the crew of any vessel with twice the manpower. Before long, every hand was proficient in his own task as well as that of his comrade. Juan wanted it this way. He recalled two occasions when he had been at sea with the Gaspars when, during a pitched sea battle with a heavily armed sloop o'war, the port side gun crew were killed when the magazine blew up. Gaspar, unable to send in replacements because the others in his crew knew nothing of manning the guns, had to abandon the pursuit and limped away. On another adventure it was necessary to send several side-boys aloft to replace the seamen who had been shot out of the rigging. The boys, unable to do the simple task of stepping the mast during the emergency, caused Gaspar to give up that chase even though he could easily have boarded the bark they were then chasing, provided he could put on enough sail to catch her. Remembering these lessons, Juan did his best to see to it that each man could double at his fellow's task in the event of an emergency.

By the twentieth of April all was in readiness for the first sea trial. Gideon, Boko, and Juan had conferred and decided to make a run down to the Dry Tortugas and back, using the cruise primarily for practice.

'And should we come across a fat merchantman?' Gideon asked, 'What d'ye expect to do then, Capitaine Juan?'

Juan smiled. 'We'll try our guns on her and use what we have learned.

'Aye,' laughed Boko. 'We'll prove ourselfs soon 'nough. As for my division, I can say they are ready and eager.'

'What do you read in the ashes?' Gideon asked Boko.

The Negro's shiny black face was grim as he replied, 'We shall find ourselfs a fat merchantman to test our guns on.'

Juan looked at the two men and grinned. 'Have your men ready to sail with the morning tide.'

That evening as Juan stood by the window in his quarters staring out at the moonlit waters of the gulf, Maha came up and leaned her head against his shoulder. During the weeks that had elapsed since Gideon's and Boko's return from Key West with the new men, she had watched a change come over Juan. He rarely spoke and when he did it was only out of necessity. She understood his mood and she knew he was preoccupied with the business of training the men and fitting out the ship. Until the first cruise he would be like this, she realized. He had a great deal on his mind – and he was worried. Although she was powerless to cope with his solemnity, nevertheless she did not give up trying.

Juan turned and looked down into Maha's rapt face. In the moonlight she looked childlike and frightened. He turned back to the window and continued staring out at the seascape, wondering at that moment why he suddenly felt as if he did not want Maha there at his side. He had decided not to take her along on the voyage but could not bring himself to the point of telling her.

'The men are going aboard the *Golden Panther*,' she said. 'Does that mean you're putting to sea in the morning?'

Juan nodded without looking at her.

'You don't want me along, do you?'

He turned again and confronted her, placing his hands upon her shoulders. 'I *do* want you with me. But perhaps next time.'

'You needn't bother explaining. I understand.'

He felt strangely guilty. He drew her near and encircled her warm body with his arms. His hands absently traced the contours of her back. Her skin felt silken and electric to the touch beneath the thin silk gown she was wearing. During the past few weeks he had not noticed that she had been making full use of the sea chest filled with beautiful clothing which he had found aboard Gaspar's ship. Suddenly, he was aware of how striking she looked. Then he realized she had been taking great pains to appear attractive to him. He felt a pleasurable warm surge envelope his body as he bent his lips to meet hers. He reached down and placed his hands upon the rounds of her buttocks beneath the gown. Her flesh was cool and yielding as his fingers probed her, caressed her, pinched her. She pressed her belly against him and wrapped her arms tightly, almost desperately, around his neck.

Juan, his hands cupping her bottom, lifted her from the floor. He walked slowly toward the bed, never for a moment removing his mouth from hers, never for a moment ceasing to breathe in her sweet breath.

He placed her gently upon the bed and knelt above her, his body now rigid and throbbing with desire. His hands swept aside the cloth of her garment as he bent his lips to her breasts, nuzzling and kissing first one, then the other, his tongue rolling around the rigid nipples in turn. Maha began to thresh her limbs and clasp her arms tighter and tighter. Little whimpers of ecstasy purled up from her lips like bubblings of froth coming to the surface from deep within. 'I love you, Juan, I love you,' she moaned, her fingers now clawing through the close-cropped hair of his scalp. 'Say you love me too.'

'I love you, Maha,' he whispered in her ear, lowering himself full length now upon her, positioning his body, taking her buttocks in both hands and holding her. Then, lifting himself eagerly, he placed his exposed member against the soft down and felt her yielding flesh, moist and warm, sucking him into her. There was a brief moment of motionlessness, then with a sudden urgency, he began to plummet into her with fierce abandon. Maha met his every stroke with a jerking thrust of her belly. They were eager and anxious and unable to control themselves. It was a violent frenzied embrace that became more and more violent with every elapsing moment until suddenly, abruptly, they each reached the pinnacle of ecstasy and felt the spasmodic climax gripping them both simultaneously.

Later, in each others' arms, Maha toyed with his upper lip, tracing a fingernail over the contours of his flesh and asked absently, 'How long will you be away, my darling?'

'As long as it takes. A few days, a week at most.'

'Will you miss me?'

'You know I shall.'

'Who will you leave on the island with me? I wouldn't like to be alone.'

'Joab will stay to guard you.'

'Do you trust him?'

'Of all the others, I trust him the most.'

'Won't you need him on the ship?'

'Joab? He's old and the old have no place on the *Golden Panther*. Besides, he has to finish making that new mains'l.'

'Oh, Juan,' she began to weep suddenly, her arms tight in desperation around his neck, 'I'm afraid. I have the strangest feeling I'll never see you again.'

Juan laughed, an attempt to dissuade her from such talk. 'Don't be an ass. Of course you'll see me again. Before you know it, I'll be back – with a surprise for you.'

'I don't want any surprises. I only want you. Please, take me with you.'

'No, it would be too dangerous. Besides, you'll be in the way.'

'No, no, I won't. I'll stay in your cabin. You won't even know I'm there.'

'I said no, and that's final.'

Maha released her arms from around his neck and turned on her back, staring at the thatched roof. In the dim moonlight shining through the window he could see tears trickling down her cheeks. Instead of drawing her to him again, Juan was unable to do so. His heart went out to her and he knew that if he should caress her he would weaken and go back on his word. Reaching for his trousers, he sat up, donned them, then strode barefoot out of the cabin.

He walked through the cool night toward the landing where the men were loading the provisions and fresh water which they were passing from hand to hand brigade fashion. Gideon and Boko looked up when Juan approached and touched their hands to their scarf-wrapped heads by way of a salute. They were setting the example they wished the crew to follow.

Juan returned their salute and went up the gangplank. He met Joab on deck, coming toward the gangway, struggling under the bulky weight of a large folded sail. Before Juan could move out of his way, Joab shifted the weight on his shoulders and said, 'Cap'n, sar. Does yo' mind if'n Ah comes 'long with y'all?'

'I would deem it a privilege to have you aboard, Joab,' Juan said diplomatically. Then, lowering his voice in a guarded aside, he said, 'But I have to leave the princess at the island and there's no one else I could trust to protect and care for her while we're off on this shakedown cruise.'

Joab seemed to grow taller as a bright smile came to his face. 'Don't yo' worry none, sar. Ol' Joab will perteck the beautiful lady with'n his life if h'it need be.'

Juan winked and patted him on the shoulder. 'I knew I could count on you. And just to make it right, if we happen upon a prize during this cruise I'll see to it personally that you get an equal share.'

'Thet's mighty gen'rous o'yo, master.'

Juan nodded. 'How many times do I have to keep telling you that I'm *not* your master and you're no longer slaves. I'm your captain, nothing more.'

Joab, chuckling to himself, shifted the load on his back and hurried toward the gangway. Juan watched him descend to the shore, then he made the rounds of the vessel. Before the crew could retire for the night everything had to be in readiness to sail with the morning tide, and though he looked carefully to find anything undone, any chore left incompleted, Juan was pleased to find nothing amiss. Gideon and Boko had done their jobs well.

Juan went into the captain's cabin and sat for a long while before the chart table that had once been Leon Gaspar's. He remembered the many years he had been Gaspar's slave, and he recalled with bitterness the thousands of hours he had been forced by his master to stand in waiting at that table, pouring wine from the decanter, as it was his duty to keep Gaspar's glass always brimming; and the hundreds of other indignities he had suffered in silence serving his master. Now that Juan was master of the vessel, he still could not forget his life as Gaspar's slave. During that moment he felt angry and disgusted with himself for having spared Gaspar's life. He felt he ought to have killed him when he had the chance and he wondered what had come over him then when he accepted Gaspar's boot kiss as payment for all the years he had been in servitude. Juan realized, as he mulled over this, that he had really expected Gaspar to defy him, to refuse to kiss his boots. He expected this and he had fully intended to kill him on the spot; but when Gaspar had begged for his life, and then had kissed his boots, he was totally unprepared for this eventuality, and so had Gideon throw him over the side.

While Juan sat contemplating the past, his thoughts returned to Maha. He wanted to have her aboard but now that he had already told her to remain on the island, and had also instructed Joab to guard her, he found he could not go back on his word no matter how much he wanted, for to do so would be a sign of weakness; and that, he could ill afford because he would lose the respect of his men. He had learned during all those years as Gaspar's slave that there was one thing a pirate captain never did: relent when once he had given a command.

One evening after Gaspar had ordered the execution of his own uncle, Pierre Gaspar, Juan had been present as usual in Gaspar's cabin – the very cabin Juan now occupied – watching as Gaspar drank himself into a stupor.

Before Gaspar finally passed out, he banged the table with his mug and told Juan, 'Know something, nigger boy? I love Pierre Gaspar because he's my uncle – my mother's brother. I don't want to string him up from the yardarm. I made a mistake, that's all. I got mad at him and I ordered him to be hung. Now I don't want to go through with it; but I can't stop the execution.'

'Why not, master? You're the captain, are you not?'

At this, Gaspar flung his mug at Juan. It struck him on the head with such force a cut was laid open. 'Let that be a lesson to you, nigger boy. A pirate captain don't take back any order once he gives it. That's the code of the brotherhood. And ye know why no order is ever took back?'

Unmindful of the blood oozing from his cut forehead, Juan had nodded.

'Because,' Gaspar went on, 'a pirate captain who takes back orders he once gives loses the respect o'his men. The men interpret such things as signs of weakness. Don't ye forget that, nigger boy.'

Juan never forgot.

He still had the scar on his forehead to remind him, and he touched it absently as he remembered.

SOMEWHERE IN THE GULF OF MEXICO
April 24, 1811
Saturday
Dawn

Within a cable's length to windward of the *Golden Panther* loomed the dark hull of a French merchantman. Juan and his crew had been chasing the lumbering vessel westward since sundown the evening before, slowly closing the gap until they were finally within range. Unfortunately for the Frenchman, the moon was full during the night and they were rarely out of sight of the *Golden Panther*'s lookouts. From the quarterdeck where he stood with glass to eye, Juan saw the merchantman's crew at quarters lighting the battle lanterns which began to glow in the gun ports as they opened them one by one until all fourteen cannons were visible.

Before the merchantman could maneuver into position to level her guns at the *Golden Panther*, Juan gave the command to the helmsman to change direction. The agile craft responded to the turn of the wheel and followed in the wake of the fleeing vessel. The distance closed fast. Aboard Juan's vessel, every man was at his post, anxious to jump at Panther John's command, chafing to get on with it, to prove worthy of their salt.

'Boko!' cried Juan, 'level your guns for a broadside. Take good aim.' Then he turned and ordered the helm brought hard aport. As the swift vessel cut across the merchantman's wake and the high defenseless stern of the ship was almost a dozen fathoms off the *Golden Panther*'s gunwales, Juan shouted, 'Fire!'

A thundering series of flames burst from the battery sending aloft to the great towering labyrinth of rigging and sails a shower of iron shot. At once the sheets began to tumble with heavy thuds to the deck. Within minutes the crippled vessel struck her colors and ran up the white flag.

A rousing cheer went up from the Negro crew as Juan

gave the command to stand by with boarding pikes and grappling hooks. Then he ordered the men to belay their weapons unless they were attacked when they went aboard. 'If they resist,' Juan shouted through the trumpet, 'show no mercy.'

The men, laughing and shouting, began to hurl the hooks across the gap and others made fast the lines. Juan, Boko, and Gideon were the first to swing aboard the vessel. Juan jumped down to the quarterdeck, pistol in one hand, cutlass in his right. He approached the captain and stood for a moment watching the man. The captain, a stout fellow in a red and blue uniform with tri-cornered cap and brass buttons, unbuckled his sword and let it drop to the deck.

Juan glared at the man. 'Pick it up and present it to me.'

With contempt in his expression, the man bent and retrieved the weapon. He held it up and then extended it to Juan.

'Who are you and where were you bound?' Juan asked when he took the weapon and glanced around to watch the crew as they disarmed the men aboard the merchantman.

'I am Capitaine Laval and I am bound for New Orleans with a cargo of silk and provisions. I don't know who you black men are, but I assure you the French Admiralty will hear of this.'

Juan laughed. 'I am Panther John. I assure you if you have any further threats to make you will not live to regret them.'

From the tone of his voice and the manner in which he stood there holding the blade against the stout captain's chest, the others in the crew who had just surrendered looked on in dread and apprehension. They did not like the surly looks of the black men who had disabled their ship and were now herding them together forward of the quarterdeck.

Gideon nodded at several of the men who at once began to order the captive crew toward the watch rail below which were the ship's longboats hanging from davits.

When the captain saw this he cried aloud, 'Murderers! We'll die out there. You can't set us adrift.'

'Why can't we?' Juan asked.

The captain's blubbery face betrayed his panic. His rheumy eyes were pale and watery as he wailed, 'The nearest land is fifty miles east of here. We'll never survive.'

'Then I shall see to it that you have provisions as well as

oars,' Juan said, turning to one of the men and ordering him to see to it that supplies and water were placed in the boats.

As the crew rowed away from their ship, the crew of the *Golden Panther* shouted and jeered. Juan, annoyed at this, at once shouted for the men to begin bringing up the cargo for transfer to their vessel. Then he went below with Gideon and Boko and began a systematic search of the ship. As they brought up sea chests and valuables they found, Gideon drew Juan aside and asked, 'Why did you spare them?'

'I saw no reason to kill them.'

Gideon's expression was difficult for Juan to fathom. He shook his head and started up the ladder toward the deck. Juan stopped him. 'You don't approve?'

'No. I didn't approve of your sparing Gaspar and I don't approve of this.'

'Would you have me turn into a butcher?'

'It would be better to be a butcher if one does not have living enemies than it is to be merciful and have enemies who will hunt you down.'

'You were the one who ordered them to their boats,' Juan said with a grin.

Gideon laughed. 'Boko's gun crew needs practice.'

Juan scratched his chin and nodded. Then he hefted the trunk he had found in the French captain's cabin to his shoulder and continued up to the deck.

It was late afternoon by the time the crew had transferred everything worth taking to the *Golden Panther* and the lines were cut loose. As they hoisted sail, Boko came aft and asked Juan for permission to give each man a ration of rum.

'First, let's see if your gun crews have learned anything. How many volleys do you think it will take to send that merchantman to the bottom?'

Juan smiled as Boko went to the rail and squinted at the vessel they were drawing away from. After several long moments of deliberation he turned and said, 'I can do it in one volley from nine guns.'

'If you do,' Juan said, 'there'll be a double ration of rum for your hands. Go to it.'

The men from the opposite side came forward to watch Boko's crews at work as Gideon steered the vessel around the crippled merchantman. Boko personally ran along the gun deck checking the elevation of every gun. When all was in readiness, and each cannon primed and fused, he stood on the bulwarks and held up a hand. The ship rode easily on the sea, wallowing just a trifle in a trough. At the exact moment when the *Golden Panther* reached the correct position with her decks aslant, Boko gave the command to fire. A volley shook the decks and shot penetrated the hull of the target just below the waterline. Within moments the ship began to list as the sea gushed into her bottom.

Juan turned and called to Tubal, 'Fetch the rum and give each man a ration. Give Boko's gunnery crew a double ration. Then we'll divide the booty here on deck.' All hands came forward and put the loot they had collected into a large pile next to the cargo which had been hoisted aboard. The men understood that the ship's cargo would later be bartered or sold at which time the proceeds from the transaction would be divided equally amongst them. Much conjecturing went on as to the amount of money the packing cases of cloth, tools, preserved foodstuffs, kegs of salt pork, barrels of sugar, hardware, and other merchandise would fetch. As the crew filled their mugs from the firkins of rum which Tubal and the two sideboys brought up to the deck, Boko and Gideon seated themselves in the midst of the crew and began the sorting out of the cutlasses, pistols, and other small arms from the general merchandise such as candlesticks, mirrors, razors, shaving mugs, clothing, boots, musical instruments, and jewelry which had been found in the sea chests and bags belonging to the crew of the captured vessel.

Even before the booty had been sorted, the men began to quarrel among themselves. When Juan saw this, he jumped down from the quarterdeck and glared round at them. 'If we're to be a brotherly crew I'll have no squabbling among you. If you men want something another man has, I suggest you trade for it. There's plenty of everything for everyone, from the looks of this pile.'

The men nodded and fell silent. Boko began to call out the names of the men and as each stepped forward, he was allowed to select three items. When every one had been called, Gideon sorted out the remaining articles and the names were called again to distribute the remainder. Despite their efforts to satisfy each man in the crew, it was obvious to Juan and his two lieutenants that there were several disgruntled blacks who felt they had been cheated and that others had received a more valuable share of the booty than had they.

Recognizing that something had to be done at once before the crew began to fight among themselves, Juan climbed up to a packing case and said to the company, 'Who among you feels he did not receive fair share?' He paused and looked around. No one replied. Juan, growing annoyed because he had seen and heard them with his own eyes and ears, repeated his question. When no one came forward he bellowed, 'You there, Felipe, and you, Pedro, step forward.'

The two men, husky Spaniards with jet black complexions, glanced round and then stepped forward. Juan, hands on his sides, fists knotted, glared at them. 'I heard both of you complaining. How say you, Pedro?'

Pedro shrugged and managed a wry smile. He held up a shaving mug and a mirror. 'Señor capitaine, sar, this be what I have. I want one those pistoles instead.'

Juan grinned. He turned round until he saw a man with three pistols stuck in his belt. 'What are you going to do with three pistols?' He paused and added, 'Do you have three hands?'

Everyone laughed. The man got the message and removed one of the mahogany-handled pistols from his belt. He sullenly pointed at the shaving mug. The trade was made and both men retired to the sidelines admiring the articles they had swapped. Juan turned to the woolly-headed Felipe and asked, 'How say you, Felipe?'

Felipe grinned and removed a gold watch from his pocket. He held it up and said, 'Me don't want this. No use to me. I want one of them,' he said, pointing at one of his fellows who was testing the sharpness of two sheath knives against his beard. When he saw what Felipe had to trade he quickly stepped toward him, extending one of the blades. Felipe seized it and held the gold watch out by the chain. The barter completed to the satisfaction of both parties, Juan looked round at the crew and asked, 'Has anyone else got a problem?'

No one uttered a word.

Juan turned and said to Gideon, 'Have the men turn to. Set a course for the Tortugas. We've a cargo to sell.'

At the order the men hastily scurried to their stations. Within minutes the vessel was bearing southward to the Dry Tortugas under full sail in a moderate breeze.

Shortly after sundown Gideon and Boko joined Juan in his cabin for their evening meal. One of the younger ex-slaves served them roast venison and porter while a second seaman who was attired in a striped shirt and pantaloons taken from one of the French sailors cranked the handle of a music box providing dinner music. Amused at the manner in which they were dining, Juan stood up and toasted his comrades. 'To the *Golden Panther* and her crew.'

'To Panther John, our capitaine!' saluted Boko and Gideon.

They drank and sat down again. Gideon turned toward the two crewmen and told them to go.

When they were alone Gideon leaned forward on the polished table and peered at Juan's face. Although he had not questioned Juan's order to set a course for the Tortugas, he had some misgivings and he said so.

Juan leaned back in his chair and lit a cigar. He handed a cigar to Boko and one to Gideon, then lifted the taper for each man to light the cigars from. When they were puffing contentedly, Juan replied to Gideon's expression of concern in a measured tone of voice. 'I know what you're thinking – that we may run into more than our share of trouble with the white buccaneers on the Tortugas. I'm aware of this. I'm also aware of two facts: one, that we can't keep hiding from Gaspar or any other white pirate. Two, sooner or later there will be a confrontation. I say that the sooner we show ourselves – and our strength – the sooner we will be in a position to go anywhere the white man goes without hiding like – like – '

'A pack of renegade wolves,' Gideon said, smiling.

'Yes,' Juan said. 'And this brings me to my next thought. If we are able to land as boldly as any white pirate crew on the Tortugas we stand an excellent chance of allying ourselves with Calico Jack and perhaps even Lafitte himself. If we are able to accomplish this, we will have nothing to fear from the Gaspars, just in case the Gaspars are trying to rally the white pirates to hunt us down. Moreover, if we show ourselves – and our strength – the white pirates who might possibly throw in with the Gaspars might just happen to stay neutral rather than run the risk of doing battle with the likes of us.'

'Well thought out,' Boko said, nodding sagely. He smiled at Gideon and then leaned forward to touch his cigar ash to a plate. Then he muttered a few words under his breath and blew upon the ashes, watching them scatter. Gideon and

Juan peered at the plate with intent interest. Boko had foretold the future too many times upon previous occasions – and had prophesied accurately – for them to dispute what he was now doing. After a long while Boko sat back and clapped his hands upon the table planks. He beamed at Juan and then smiled at Gideon. Then he said in his rich basso, 'Thar will be trouble, but we will batten 'em at their own game, mateys.' He laughed heartily and added, 'Beware the white cockade. We will make our mark and the white pirates will think twice afore they pesters with the likes o'us black men.'

'What's this about a white cockade?' Juan inquired, frowning.

Boko drew on his cigar and removed it from his thick lips. He studied the tip for several moments and said, 'Ol' Boko ain't so sure 'bout thet. Just beware that's all.'

Juan frowned at Gideon. Gideon shrugged and then pushed himself away from the table. He arose and hooked his thumbs over his belt. 'Gentlemen,' he said, 'we've come a long way these past few weeks since we escaped the Gaspars. I mean to keep things the way they are. Living the life of a white gentleman and ship's officer is to my liking.'

Both Juan and Boko agreed. It was a point upon which there would be no dispute.

Shortly before three o'clock the following day, Sunday, the twenty-fifth of April, the *Golden Panther* dropped anchor off Loggerhead Key in the Dry Tortugas beside two vessels, one of which was a sloop, the other a barkentine flying Lafitte's burgee. Juan and his lieutenants stood at the watchrail looking the vessels over as the crew lowered the gig after the sails had been furled and the anchors secured so the ship would swing free and easy on her moorings in the stiff breeze then whipping up frothy white caps upon the sea out of the northeast. Shutting his spyglass, Juan handed it to Boko as he took the man-ropes of the poop ladder as he stepped over the side.

'Keep a sharp weather eye peeled,' Juan said as he descended. 'If Gideon and I haven't returned by eight bells tonight, send a party ashore under arms to fetch us.'

Boko smiled and nodded.

Gideon stepped over the rail after checking his weapons and climbed down to the gig. Tubal and two husky seamen hoisted the small sail and put the gig about, steering a course for the shore landing.

When they moored the boat alongside a lugger which was tied to a rickety pier several bewiskered white men came down to the shore to watch them. Juan and Gideon nodded cordially but the men gave them contemptuous looks. With a smile curling his upper lip, Juan went up to them and asked, 'Can you gentlemen tell us where we might find Lafitte's capitaine?'

'What do a nigger want'n with Lafitte's capitaine?'

Juan continued smiling. His hand closed over the hilt of his cutlass. He said, without a waver in his tone, 'That's my business. Now unless you want to cross blades with me, suppose you answer my question.'

The men scowled, but after sizing up Juan, Gideon, and the other three, shrugged and pointed at a building several hundred yards north of where they were standing. They backed away and turned and walked slowly in the opposite direction.

Gideon laughed. He fell into step beside Juan and the others followed them. They reached the crudely built long-house and entered through a slatted door to find themselves in a smoke filled room which was arranged after the fashion of the times like a country tavern. Fifteen white men were seated at rough hewn tables about the place. At the far end of the room beside a smoking hearth in which several ducks were roasting on spits above the coals, was a makeshift bar consisting of a plank resting upon two grog barrels. Standing at the bar with tankards in their hands were two tall men in garish red and gold trimmed coats. The men were more elaborately dressed than anyone else present. The others at the tables were attired in ordinary seaman's clothing. When the two at the bar saw the five Negroes enter, they turned round and watched as they approached.

Juan stopped in the center of the room and confronted the two. 'I am Capitaine Juan Gomez of the *Golden Panther*. Might either of you gentlemen be the master of that barkentine flying Lafitte's burgee?'

'Aye,' the taller of the two men said, stepping forward and eyeing Juan curiously. 'You're talking to him. I'm Capitaine François Decroix of the *Le Homard*.' He clicked the heels of his boots but did not bow. 'What do you want?'

'I want to send a message to Jean Lafitte,' Juan said,

producing a small scroll from a pocket. 'Would you do me the honor, sir?'

'And what would be the nature of this letter?'

Juan stood his ground. He confronted the white captain without a sign of backing down. 'What I have written is for Jean Lafitte's eyes alone.'

'You – a nigger who can write.'

'I am a man. I am capitaine of the *Golden Panther*, not a nigger.' He handed the sealed letter to Decroix.

From the tone of Juan's voice and the steadfast manner in which he stood his ground, hand upon the hilt of his cutlass, Decroix was forced either to draw his weapon or else change his tack. He doffed his white plumed cap and with a click of his boot heels, bowed with a flourish. 'I beg your pardon, m'sieu. You are the first Negro capitaine I have ever met.'

Gideon stepped forward and doffed his tri-cornered cap. 'You will not forget my capitaine, sar. He is Panther John.'

A spark of recognition flickered in Decroix' eyes as he straightened up and snapped his fingers. Then he turned and pointed at Juan. 'You are the slave of Leon Gaspar who rebelled and stole one of his ships, are you not?'

'I am Panther John. I spared Gaspar's life.'

'Yes, sar,' said Gideon, nodding, 'that he did. He threw Gaspar over the side instead of slitting his throat.'

'Mon dieu! Is this the truth?'

Juan nodded. 'It is the truth. Gaspar kissed my boots and begged for mercy.'

The men in the room, listening intently, looked on in amazement. Decroix and the officer with him exchanged amused glances. Then Decroix said, 'This confirms what we've heard. So Gaspar – the great Gasparilla himself – kissed his nigger's boots. Well, what do you know, mon dieu!'

Juan continued to stand without moving. He glared at the white men and said, 'This is the last time I intend to remind you – we are free men – *not* niggers.'

'I beg your pardon, m'sieu. It shan't happen again.' He then turned and said round to the others in the room, 'This is Capitaine Panther John. He is not a nigger and his men are not niggers. They are gentlemen buccaneers like ourselves.' With that, Decroix once again faced Juan, drawing a snuff box from his waistcoat. 'Mon capitaine,' he said with a show of gold teeth, 'does that please you?'

Juan nodded. To have achieved this much was a small victory. He boldly walked up to the plank and snapped his fingers at the innkeeper. 'A round of grog for everyone.'

The innkeeper made no move until he saw the fistful of gold pieces Juan slapped down upon the plank bar. Then he hastened to do his bidding. The others in the room crowded to the bar, tankards in their hands, standing in line at the keg tap.

Decroix tapped the letter Juan had given him against his cheek, then with an elaborate gesture, demonstrated that he was placing it inside his coat. 'I shall see to it that Lafitte gets this personally. Will there be any other messages you'd care to have relayed?'

'No,' Juan said, 'but there is something you might tell me. We have aboard a certain quantity of fine silks and cloth and other mercantile articles. We would like to barter them for powder and shot – or perhaps sell them for gold.'

'What else have you for sale?'

Juan smiled cryptically. 'When we have disposed of this lot, we'll have others to barter or sell.'

'And I take it you intend to obtain these cargoes from generous merchants?'

'Oui,' Juan laughed.

'Come, Panther John,' Decroix said. 'Sit with me at yon table. You're a man after my own heart.' With that, he clapped a hand around Juan's shoulder and they walked toward the table.

Gideon, Tubal, and the two seamen mingled with the others in the tavern. Before long an air of geniality pervaded the atmosphere. As Juan sat drinking with Decroix, he was aware of a quality of hostility in the manner of several of the seamen present. But later, when he looked around to see what they were up to, he noticed they had left the establishment. One of the Negro seamen in Juan's company had vanished too.

Shortly before eight bells, Juan arose and called Gideon. Then the two men joined the crewman and went to look for the missing Negro. They strolled down to the moorings, got a lantern from the gig, and went off to search in earnest for the man. Later, as they were returning to the tavern again, still searching, they found him, staggering drunk, sprawling and stumbling to his feet, trying to make his way toward them.

When they reached his side the man passed out. Gideon and the sailor lifted him and carried him bodily to the gig. Then they signaled the *Golden Panther* they were returning by waving the lantern, and cast off.

PANTHER CAY
April 27, 1811
Tuesday
Noon

As soon as the crew had lowered the gangplank, even before the vessel had been moored to the lines on shore, Juan hurried from the ship and began to run toward the shelters. During the two hours it had taken the *Golden Panther* to navigate the shoals on their aproach to the island, a powerful sense of foreboding had gripped Juan, and then his crew. Even Boko had admitted he sensed something awry; but exactly what he sensed, he would not say. He admitted only that Juan would see 'what ye will see'. After this was said, Juan ordered Gideon to fire the cannon. When this was done, and there still had been no response to their signal or any sign of life, Juan climbed to the crow's nest and scanned the island through the glass. From that distance it was impossible to tell what was wrong. As the vessel drew within a cable's length of the landing, Juan detected a faint wisp of smoke ashore coming from his quarters. At the sight of this he felt suddenly sick at the stomach. He swung down the mainsheet, tossed his glass to one of the men, and rushed down the gangplank with but one thought in his mind: Maha. Why hadn't she or Joab shown themselves?

Just when he reached the clearing, Juan saw what was left of the shelters – and of Joab. The man was staked out on the ground, his limbs tied fast to timbers. A sword was sticking up out of his rotund belly and a pool of drying blood encircled him.

Juan dropped to his knees beside Joab and listened to his chest for some sign of life. He detected a faint beat and gently patted Joab's cheeks. The elderly Negro's eyes opened. He stared blankly at Juan and muttered feebly, 'H'it was Gaspar's men. They come heah in a sloop. Flying a white cockade. Took us by surprise they did. Maha, I made her hide in a tree. They tortured me. One man, he said he found out this island from nigger – drunk – on Tortugas. They said Gaspar will pay thousand pieces of gold for your head – five hundred for Maha's head. I tried stop them, but they, they . . .'

Juan shrank away from the dying man. He stood up and spun around. Then he broke into a run as Gideon and the others in the crew came upon the scene. Juan rushed into the longhouse and halted abruptly in the doorway. Inside the smoking ruins of the quarters at the window he saw Maha's nude body. She had been decapitated, her head severed just below the jaw leaving only the gory remains of her neck and throat. He stared at the sight, shaking violently, retching, staggered at the horror of it. Then he turned away, weeping, groans of agony rumbling in his chest. He went outside and stood swaying in the sunlight. Gideon and the others came running over. Juan blinked at them through his tears. Then he saw the Negro crewman, the one who had got drunk with the white sailors on Tortugas. Without a word, Juan drew his blade and moved woodenly toward the man. Before anyone realized what he was doing, Juan began to lunge at him, slashing the cutlass wildly. He decapitated the man with one blow and continued to chop at his corpse even before it had stopped jerking and rolling on the ground.

Like a man berserk, Juan turned and confronted his crew, the blood and gore dripping from his blade which he waved in his hand.

'This bilge rat was the one who betrayed us. Let this be a reminder to all of you that no one betrays Panther John. Now let's go men! I've a score to settle. I want Maha's head back.'

The men who had ventured into the longhouse and saw the gory sight, emerged screaming with rage. In a body everyone ran down to the landing and began to clamber aboard the ship. Gideon barked orders at the top of his voice as everyone in both divisions worked to send the vessel racing after the sloop which they reasoned had only a few hours' lead.

Under full canvas the vessel careened over the labyrinth of shoals, heading for blue water. Juan, still clutching the blood-smeared cutlass in his fist, paced the quarterdeck like a black panther, impatient to slake his lust for revenge. Every quarter hour or so he would shout up at the lookouts to ask if they had sighted anything. Then he cried, 'A hundred pieces of eight to the first man who spies the *White Cockade*!'

Every man not on duty at his station went aloft to scan the horizon. Gideon and Boko, standing beside the helm, watched the compass as the helmsman steered a course for Gasparilla Island where they knew the sloop they were chasing was headed.

Although he felt sick at the stomach and his head was pounding fiercely, Juan continued his nervous pacing without a pause. It was not until four by the clock that afternoon that the lookout atop the main cried out, 'Sail ho! Two points off the starboard bow.'

All hands rushed to look. Juan flung down his cutlass with such force the point buried itself in the deck. Then he seized a line and swung down from the quarterdeck to the main where he grabbed the line and went up, hand over hand.

The moment he spied the sloop through the lookout's glass, Juan shouted down to the crew, 'Break out the small arms. I want every man armed to the teeth. You there, look alive and make ready the guns. Load and prime the cannon with iron. I want that goddamn hell ship demasted and when we board her, I'd better see every head rolling on her decks!'

The crew looked up at Juan and shouted with excitement. Juan's voice was heard above all others as he yelled down to Tubal, 'Break out the rum and give every man a double ration.'

By six o'clock the *White Cockade* was but a nautical mile ahead of the *Golden Panther*, her deck alive with men, her sails almost slack in the feeble breeze. The lighter canvas sails of Juan's ship remained filled and this fact alone enabled them to overtake the white pirates' vessel. As they approached on a shallow tack, Juan could see one of the two men who had been at Tortugas standing at her after-rail, peering at them through a glass.

The moment they were within range, Juan held his cutlass aloft as every man in the starboard battery stood ready by their cannons which had been loaded with grape, roundshot, and canister. Boko, standing beside Juan, suddenly cried, 'Ready . . . Fire!'

Juan swung the blade down and the gunners lowered their flames. One by one the cannon thundered, delivering an almost simultaneous fusillade of flaming destruction. Even before the cannon had ceased smoking they were loaded and primed again. Again Boko gave the command and again Juan dashed down his blade in a signal to the gun crews. In reply, the pirates aboard the sloop peppered the crew of the *Golden Panther* with volley after volley of musket balls which they fired from the poop and forecastle. The vessel was not in position to train her guns on the pursuer and Juan had no intention of permitting this. He barked commands at the crew aloft and at the helmsman which sent the swift vessel across the *White Cockade*'s wake and back around again to the port side where her guns would be ineffective. The volley of cannonade demasted the vessel, and the second volley shot away the stern and the rudder. When the fires aboard the crippled ship began to rage out of control, Juan gave the command to board her and the crew along the rails began heaving their grappling hooks and boarding pikes. Juan led his crew across to the deck of the sloop, chopping with his cutlass like a black demon on a rampage. He recognized one of the two sailors he had seen at Loggerhead Key and shouted to the others to let him be. Then Juan rushed him, dirk in one hand, cutlass in the other. He parried and thrust and lunged, driving the man into the watchrail. With a furious slash of his blade he disarmed him and then held the point of his weapon against the man's throat. 'Now you will pay for what you did to the princess!'

'Quarter!' screamed the man. 'Quarter! I didn't do it. It was Raoul. He was the one. He raped her and then he cut off her head.'

'Where's this Raoul?' screamed Juan.

The man flicked his eyes in the direction of a tall red-bearded man who was standing atop a hatch, blade in hand, fighting off three of Juan's crew. Juan stepped back, drove the point of his cutlass through the man's throat, then jumped down to the hatch and called to his crew to let the white man be. 'He's mine!' Juan shouted, parrying the man's blade and then driving step by step toward him with expertly flashing blade. Just as Juan found an opening and buried the point of his cutlass in the man's chest, two others jumped down to the hatch, swords in hand, and began to attack from both sides at once. Juan whirled around. In a crouch, he sallied forth and went under the first man's blade to drive home his weapon in the man's stomach. He withdrew and spun lightly around like a dancer, then came up toward the other man, blade flashing in the twilight like burnished blood-red copper. Minutes later every white man lay dead.

The crew of the *Golden Panther* ransacked the burning vessel and then returned across the bulwarks, cutting loose the lines. As they drifted away in a calm sea, Juan stood by the starboard cannons himself, firing each gun in turn, sending round shot into the hull until no hull was left and only debris floated on the water's surface.

When he finally turned away from the guns, Juan dropped his cutlass and walked stiff-legged down to his cabin. He opened the door and entered, then stumbled across a box someone had placed in the center of the floor.

Cursing, Juan climbed to his feet. He peered at the box and went over to it. Just as he reached down to lift the lid Boko entered the cabin.

'No, don't tech thet thar box, Juan. H'it Maha's head.'

At this, Juan sank to his knees sobbing. He threw his arms around the box and drew it to him. For a long while he remained thus, frozen, weeping, suffering a pain he had never before known.

The next morning Gideon and Boko entered Juan's cabin and found him sitting at the planked mahogany table with the box containing Maha's head before him. Boko poured some white powder into the tankard and Gideon mixed it with rum. They spoke to Juan several times, but the young man would not reply. Finally Boko picked up the drink and held it to Juan's lips. Juan drank, though he seemed not to be aware of what he was doing. When the cup was empty, Boko and Gideon pulled Juan away from the table and led him to his bunk where they pressed him back, covered him, and then removing the box containing the grisly remains of the woman Juan had so desperately loved, they went out.

As they walked along the passageway toward the quarters they shared, Gideon asked Boko, 'Did you see all this written in the ashes too?'

Boko smiled at Gideon. It was a knowing smile, one without humor. 'Oui, I saw it.'

'Then why did you not try to prevent it from happening? You might have warned us and we might have spared the princess' and Joab's lives if we would've returned in time.'

Boko lowered the box containing the severed head to the deck. He covered it with a blanket and pushed it into a corner of the cabin. Then, on bended knee, he looked up at Gideon and replied, 'One does not turn back the tides. Fate is a tide and no man can change it.'

PANTHER CAY
April 27, 1821
Saturday
Dawn

Juan sat at the desk in his quarters staring through blood-shot eyes at the ten log books before him which he had spent the entire night reading. For the first time since Maha's death a decade before, Juan had taken time out to think over the events and deeds of his life, and for the first time he realized he could no longer refrain from facing up to reality as he had been doing all that time. Shortly after Maha's death he began to keep a log in which he recorded faithfully everything he and his crew did. As the days passed into weeks, and the weeks into months and years, Juan remained dedicated but to one calling: that of a pirate captain whose only thought was to lead his men, and to prove his crew of all-Negro pirates to be better than any white crew afloat. Each night before retiring Juan had dutifully entered into his thick log books long accounts of the events and actions which had taken place during the day. He entered everything of consequence, no matter how minute, from the minutes and degrees of their position at sea to the number of white men killed each day while in the act of boarding and capturing vessels on the high seas. He also entered detailed inventories of the goods seized, the powder and shot expended, the specie and bullion taken and buried on Panther Cay and other hiding places in the Florida Keys, as well as the names of his men who fell in battle or who died of illness and disease.

Everything was entered except his private thoughts – the thoughts and memories of the loved one Gaspar's men had taken from him – the tortured thoughts of what might have been – his unborn child Maha was carrying at the time of her murder – the laughter and the tears they might have shared together. All this Juan did not need to record in his journals for it was unnecessary. In his mind and in his heart he lived again and again the beautiful moments he had spent with Maha, his princess. Except for when he was occupied with the business of capturing victims at sea and doing battle with those who resisted, Juan could not escape his memories. Occasionally, he had tried to drown his memories in drink, but this rendered him unfit to lead his men and since he felt so strongly the responsibility for them, this avenue of escape could not be open to him. He preferred being occupied with the adventure and excitement of living by cannon and sword to that of any other way of life; hence, ten years had slipped by since Maha's death, and now, in his thirtieth year, Juan had arrived at an age in life when he could no longer disregard the urges within that had made him into the tireless, restless freebooter and hater of white men that he was. No longer did he savor the tart edge of dangerous living; no longer did he enjoy flirting with death; for now he felt the need to savor and to treasure life rather than flaunt it perilously.

Something about the warm sunlight streaming through the open window that morning reminded him of another day in another place five years before. He and his men had landed a few miles up the coast from a plantation in Martinique. From there they trekked along the beach until they reached the plantation. They crept up to the big house through the cane fields and attacked it, felling the mulatto guards and the white people who lived and worked there as overseers with musket and cutlass as they closed in a tightening circle like a noose of raging humanity closing upon helpless victims. Juan had been the first to enter the house, blood dripping from his cutlass. He surprised the elderly planter who had been sitting at his polished mahogany desk and ended his life with a single blow of the blade. As the crew ransacked the building in search of the treasure which was said to be there, Juan seated himself at the planter's desk and fingered through the account books, wondering what it would be like to be a gentleman so rich and so elegant. It was then that Gideon rushed into the drawing room where Juan was sitting to announce that they had found two buried chests in the yard behind the house which contained a king's ransom in specie and silver bullion. The crew rounded up the sixty-five slaves who lived and worked on the plantation and marched them back to the ship after putting the torch to the fields and buildings. Except for the household effects, silver service, candelabra, and numerous trunks of clothing, jewelry, clocks, and other valuables, only two articles of furniture were toted back to the *Golden Panther* on the backs of the slaves. These were the planter's polished walnut desk and the brocade upholstered arm chair that matched it.

It was in that chair that Juan Gomez sat that morning in April of 1821, contemplating his past.

He recalled with no little amusement the events of that day when the Negro slaves were brought aboard the ship. Boko and Gideon were the first to select two pretty wenches out of the lot and the rest of the crew followed suit, each man choosing a wench to his taste. Of the sixty-five slaves taken, forty-six were prime females ranging in age from thirteen to twenty-nine. The rest were boys and men who meekly stood in a single file along the deck awaiting their fate. Of the forty-three men in the crew at that time, only several were not pleased with the women they had selected and a few minor quarrels erupted. Juan was quick to call a halt to the bickering, taking it upon himself to shuffle the couples until every man was, for the moment, satisfied. Of course, Juan being the captain had the pick of the women; but to the surprise of his men he did not choose one, but three, which he at once sent to his cabin and ordered to bathe themselves.

Several days later Juan had called a meeting between Boko, Gideon, Tubal, and several of the others whom he had promoted, and they decided amongst themselves that a pirate ship was no place for women. The crew not only became lackadaisical, neglecting their duties and tasks, but they also became quarrelsome and overtly envious of each other. During the first day out of Martinique there had been three duels, the result of which one man had been lost overboard and two others were badly wounded. The second day one crew member was murdered in his sleep and two others went berserk, chasing each other about the ship with dirks and cutlasses, wreaking havoc aboard the vessel and nearly killing themselves when they decided to finish their duel fifty feet above the deck hanging from the mizzen while slashing at each other.

The vessel put in at Havana and the slaves were promptly marched to the market where they were sold at a handsome price. The first wenches to be sold under the hammer were Juan's. He wanted to set the example and he succeeded. The next day when the ship was making the Windwards out of Havana the crew agreed Juan and their leaders had made the best decision and they were all close as brothers again, no longer at each others' throats.

Juan, sitting at his desk, idly thumbed through the pages of his log books, recalling to mind the incidents which stood out most in memory. His finger stopped the riffling of pages in the book which marked his near-confrontation with Leon Gaspar at Tortugas in 1812. Fortunately for both Gaspar and Juan, Jean Lafitte had thrown in with the Americans and had got all the other freebooters then sailing the Caribbean and the Gulf of Mexico to do likewise in order to help fight the British on the side of the States of America. This pact required that during the conflict, all previous and outstanding vendettas between the rival pirate leaders and their crews were from that time forth to be buried. Each pirate chieftain who signed the pact, also swore allegiance to the brotherhood.

On the day when Capitaine Juan Gomez signed the pact at Tortugas, just as he was drinking a toast with the other captains, in walked Leon and Don Jose Gaspar. For a long moment the white men and the black man stared at each other, their hands on their cutlasses. Every man in the tavern on Loggerhead Key held his breath, watching the confrontation, knowing that Panther John had vowed to have Gasparilla's head just as Gasparilla had likewise made such a vow.

The moment before blades were drawn, Jean Lafitte arose from the table and stepped between them. He laughed in that genteel way of his and gallantly waved the Gaspar brothers toward the table where the document and quills were awaiting them. Still hurling murderous glances at Juan over their shoulders, the two French pirates signed the parchment scroll and raised their hands to swear their allegiance to the brotherhood and to Jean Lafitte. When this business was done, all tankards were raised and a toast was drunk to seal the bargain. From that moment on, the pirates had become privateer captains who had pledged themselves to make war on the British but to spare, for the duration, all American and allied shipping. Moreover, Lafitte made it clear that all those who joined were to forget their grudges against each other and also that they were to take their orders from him until the conflict was over.

Juan and his lieutenants, Boko and Gideon, stood apart from the white men, watching as they pranced about, drinking and boasting of their deeds, and in general, excluding the black men from their society. It was at this time that Juan realized the other captains were not ignoring him because he was black; but rather because he was a newcomer and an upstart to their midst who had to prove his salt before they would accept him as one of their own kind. Until that moment, Juan had not realized he would be required to earn a place in their esteem by deeds, not by words. And it was at that moment, in the presence of the Lafittes, the Decroix', (who did not deliver Juan's letter to Lafitte the year before requesting a letter of marque), the Gaspars, Calico Jacks, Hanging Hughs, and the other buccaneers of infamy, that Panther John first came to understand he would never belong to their society regardless of his vow of allegiance to, and membership in, the brotherhood.

On that morning in April, 1821, so many years after the War of 1812 had been won by the Americans, and so many years after the brotherhood had more or less disbanded with each crew of cutthroats and pirates going their own merry way, Juan contemplated his own future. His pirate band had grown to seventy good men and true, all Negroes, all fierce fighting men, all crafty seamen who knew their business; and all chafing to go to sea again and again to do battle just for the sake of a good fight, and just for the excitement of taking a rich prize. Of late it had been increasingly more difficult to find and capture likely merchantmen for two reasons: one, because the growing fleet of the American Navy patroled the coastal waters with increasing effectiveness and on more than one occasion they had just barely made it where the deep draft vessels could not pursue them to their hideout at Panther Cay; and two, the merchantmen were heavily armed and manned with experienced crews who knew how to defend their vessels.

The original *Mer Jewel* which they had renamed the *Golden Panther* had long since been replaced with a swifter and larger vessel of twenty-six guns which they called simply the *Panther*. And now, after nearly two months of inactivity, of fruitless sailing the waters of the Gulf and the Caribbean in search of likely prizes, Juan and his men were more restless than ever. It was time to venture into bluer waters where fatter and richer prizes would be theirs for the taking, and where there was less chance of being caught by double or triple-decked men o'war. The question was, did they dare venture into the mid-Atlantic and attack the vessels plying the trade routes between the States and Europe?

Juan was not for it. He knew the risks and the perils only too well of what it meant for a crew of such numbers to be pent up at sea aboard ship for weeks and months at a time. He knew only too well that the rewards of such efforts would hardly be worthwhile.

As he sat thinking, his mind wandering over the events of the past, Juan remembered again the easy fast money they had been paid when they sold their first cargo of slaves, the slaves they had taken from the plantation at Martinique which they sold in Havana. And he remembered a second time, when they sold eighteen prime blacks in the market at New Orleans less than a year before. They received more for the slaves on that last voyage than they had received for the combined cargoes of six cargoes they had pirated on the high seas.

It was while he was deliberating these economics that Boko suddenly appeared in the doorway and gently knocked on the ajar door. 'Cap'n Juan,' he said, venturing into the room with his usual familiar swagger, 'Me and Gideon been tawkin' things over and we got a idear.'

Juan nodded at a chair beside the windows. Boko went over to it and sat down, stretching out his long legs, digging his boot heels into the nap of a calfskin rug spread upon the puncheon floor. He deliberated several moments before speaking as if about to broach a matter of great delicacy. 'This here idear we's got come up when I was reading the ashes.'

'You haven't done that in years.'

Boko chuckled. 'Warn't much call for prophecies of late.'

'What's the call now?'

The big man scratched his head. For the first time Juan noticed how grey Boko had become. It seemed he had aged years since he had last noticed.

'*Well?*' he asked, growing impatient at Boko's hesitation.

'Things been too peaceable of late, kind o'like the calm when they's gonna be a storm. So,' he drew a deep breath and clapped his gnarled brown hands together with a crisp slap, 'I figgered it was high time I told the ashes.'

'And what did you read in them?'

'That we gonna change our way o'living. Thet we's gonna settle ourselfs down and raise ourselfs famblies. I kind of like thet thar idear, don't you? Having a good woman to look after you and all like thet, might be comfortsome.'

Juan grinned. 'I've thought about it too.'

'I know,' Boko said. 'Me and Gid, we been keeping a eye on you. Cap'n Juan, you ain't getting no younger neither. You could do with a good woman to keep your back scratched cold nights.'

Juan laughed. 'Will you stop bandying about and get to the point? I think I get what you're driving at, but I'd rather you tell me.'

Boko slapped his knees and chuckled. He cocked his head at Juan somewhat in a fatherly way and said, 'We tawked up a storm we did. We got to figgering too. We figgered it warn't much profit nowadays in pirating. The old days is behind us now. We think we oughter try our hand where the big money is at.'

'Which is?'

'Slaving.'

'We did some of that, didn't we?'

'What was thet bunch from Martinique and the other coffle we sold in 'Orleans? Thet was just pankying around. Me and Gid, we tawked about goin' whole hog. Straight to Africy and cotch ourselfs primes what ain't broke to white man's ways yet.'

'I thought about that too,' Juan said.

'We figgered you did.'

Juan and Boko studied each other for a time. It was as if both men were measuring each other, trying to fathom the other's thoughts. The question was, which man knew the other best?

Juan smiled. He closed the log book on the top of the stack before him and put his boots up on the polished top of the desk. 'What have you and Gid in mind?'

'We turns loose about two-thirds of our hands. With about twenty hands and ourselfs, we can load the *Panther* with right smart provisions and set a course for the Gold Coast. If we gets about a hundred prime niggers we oughter get a thousand a head up at Natchez.'

'That means smuggling them into the States,' Juan said.

'Since the embargo on imported Negroes, things has been rough for slavers, you know that.'

'And since when do a embargo stop Panther John?'

Juan laughed. 'The Americans have imposed a death penalty on slavers who are caught bringing Africans into the country.'

'So what? Piracy is punish'ble by death too, h'ain't h'it?'

'Touché.'

'An' whilst we is out in the Atlantic if'n we comes across a likely prize, h'ain't no reason why we can't help ourselfs, is they?'

Juan stood up abruptly and leaned against the open window. He peered out at the Gulf of Mexico and the shimmering horizon beyond, remembering other moments when he had gazed out at the blazing nothingness of sea and sky and rising sun of morning. His life had been empty since Maha had been taken from him and perhaps the time had come for him to change his way of life. Was it time now for a new day to dawn in the life of Captain Juan Gomez, the dreaded Panther John?

Juan turned and frowned at Boko. 'There's another reason why you're here this morning, isn't it?'

Boko smiled. He looked weary and old beyond his years. He drew a deep breath and clutched the arms of the chair as if to support himself. 'Aye, Cap'n. Tubal just returned to the island in the gig. He was visiting his woman over at Matecumbe Cay and he picked up a piece of news.'

'Bad news?'

'Not good. It seems you been cheated out o'your revenge on Gaspar. The *Enterprise* blasted his ship to kingdom come. He went down with her off Charlotte Harbor whilst he was making a run for it.'

'Why the hell was he running?'

'I was getting to thet. Tawk is thet the States of America is taking over Florida come next year. H'it's gettin' too hot for buccaneers like us to make a honest livin' in these here warters any more.'

'And if we turn to slaving that'll mean we'll be on the move all the time and there'll be less risk of getting caught by the American navy?'

Boko stood up and went over to Juan. He put his arm around the young man's shoulders and laughed. 'Now you got the idear.'

Juan smiled and embraced Boko. 'All right. Let's clear out of here. Dig up the chests and divide the booty and let's shove off for Key West. We can put the men ashore there.'

'No, it's too hot down thar, and I don't mean weather-wise. Let's carry 'em as far as Havana and desert 'em thar. No use stickin' our necks out to do them blackguards a good turn.'

With a nod, Juan agreed. He walked Boko to the door and told him on parting, 'Don't say anything to the men. When we get to Havana, keep aboard all those you and Gideon want with us. Let the rest go ashore. We'll be long gone before they realize they've been beached for good.'

'How about the irons?'

'What irons?'

'We'll need a couple tons o'leg irons and whatnot to chain them niggers in the holds.'

Juan nodded in denial. 'No. It's bad enough to sell our own color flesh. I won't see them chained in coffles or mistreated in any way. And another thing, make certain enough stores and quinine and black-strap is put aboard. I remember like it was yesterday the slaver that brought me to this part of the world. They were dying like flies all around me. There wasn't enough food and no medical treatment. What with the scurvy and diarrhea and jungle rot, it was no wonder so many had to be pitched over the side. I won't be responsible for such as that, not on my ship.'

Boko shook his head slowly from side to side. 'A slaver is gotta have a iron belly. You gotta be hard. Remember, them niggers is savages. You can't be lax with 'em, or else they'll mutiny. I heard tell o'thet happening a couple times.'

'Maybe so,' Juan said, keeping his voice low to prevent the men who were just beginning to awaken and stir about the compound from hearing, 'but my conditions are what I want observed – or else – '

Boko drew away a step and looked Juan up and down. He smiled and said, 'Cap'n, whatever you say.'

SOMEWHERE IN THE ATLANTIC OCEAN
June 13, 1821
Wednesday
3 p.m.

The crew had been watching the frigate's sails since she had first been spotted on the horizon early that morning. Hour after hour they had gained on the vessel until they were close enough now to make out her insignia and definitely establish that she was a British merchantman.

'What do you make of her?' Gideon asked Juan as he stood resting his spyglass on the cavil of the main boom while peering at the vessel they were rapidly overtaking.

'From the looks of that wide beam, those twelve guns, and the bales of cargo on deck, it's pretty and obvious: she's bound for England, probably with her coffers full of gold and her holds swollen with rich goods.'

'How many men can you see aboard?'

Juan shrugged. 'It appears to me the men are Royal Navy.'

'Marines?'

'No. Ordinary seamen. About forty, more or less.'

'That's a relief. I'm getting too old to be ducking musket balls.'

Juan grunted and handed the glass to Gideon as he glanced aloft at the sails and called to the crew in the rigging to trim the royals and flying jib. Close-hauled as the *Panther* was, making a steady ten knots, the spray flying well up the weather leech of the foresail, the vessel slowly, steadily, gained on the frigate.

By four p.m. the frigate was barely three miles dead ahead, jammed on the wind and trying to brace her head-yards sharper and lie nearer the wind than her pursuer.

Two hours later they were close enough to see the striped uniforms of the seamen and the brass buttons glinting in the late afternoon sun on the first mate's coat. Gideon wanted Juan to begin pitching shot at the frigate from the long eighteen they had in the weather bridle-port; but to this request Juan adamantly refused. 'We'll lose a cable's length and more if we yaw off to fire. Never mind you now, we'll be near enough soon to send a broadside into her.'

From the top gallant forecastle, Juan, Gideon, and Boko stood watching everything which took place aboard the frigate, amused as the crew was seen reeving fresh gear on deck, putting on a seizing to a traveler on the jibstay, and sending aloft men to hurriedly stitch chafing mats on the lee backstays while others worked aft and amidships shinnying up the shrouds with tin pots around their necks, greasing the main-gaff jaws and shaking the wrinkles now and again out of the gaff tops'l or the mizzen. Abaft of the British frigate's taffrail stood two men in fancy dress uniforms, both of whom took turns with a quadrant in their hands calculating the distance between the two vessels. One man nervously paced the deck, going to the binnacle now and again, then to examine a chart spread upon the deck at his feet which he would pore over closely with a pair of dividers in his hands.

Juan was not idle aboard the *Panther*. When the breeze lulled he ordered the lower rigging slacked up and had all extra weight and hamper from the tops got down. Then he sent the crew below struggling under the weight of heavy round shot which he ordered to be placed in their hammocks, and sent Boko to move several of the carronades about the spardeck until the ship was in the best sailing trim.

Gideon reported that their position was approximately two hundred ninety nautical miles east of Puerto Rico. 'There'll be a full moon most of the night.' Gideon added with a touch of amusement, 'so we ought to have our quarry in sight the night through.'

From past experience, Gideon knew it was unwise to overtake and board a victim at sea at twilight. With an unfamiliar deck underfoot in the growing darkness, a fighting crew, no matter how experienced, cannot be expected to excel in such an endeavor.

'As near as I can reckon,' Juan told Gideon later, 'there're forty hands aboard yon frigate, outnumbering us two to one.'

Gideon laughed. He waved a hand and said, 'Then why don't we pull that same trick we used when we captured that Spaniard with a full company of troops back in '15?'

With a smile Juan nodded. Then, just as they were drawing within range while overtaking the towering hulk of an old galleon, to their dismay they saw the vessel was a troop transport. Instead of firing at the vessel with round shot when they came within cannon range, they lobbed fiery cannister doused with whale oil at the big ship's rigging. In a panic, the troops were dispersed from the rails and put to work in bucket brigades to fight the fires. The pirates boarded the burning vessel and captured the demoralized crew and passengers of armed soldiers with only a few shots being fired and only one man being wounded.

After Juan thought it over he nodded slowly and said, 'No, I'd prefer taking her intact. It appears to me she's laden with tobacco and cotton. It'd be a shame to lose that cargo should the fire get out of hand. Besides, I rather like the lines of that frigate.' He paused and eyed Gideon curiously. 'If we take her, how'd you like to be her master?'

Gideon's rotund brown face was devoid of expression as he blinked and made no immediate reply. Somehow the thought had never entered his mind to command his own ship. Finally, Gideon shrugged and said, 'No, Cap'n Juan. Thank you, no. I'm too old for such a chore.'

'It was an idea.'

'Yes, that it was. But being as how we're headed for Sierra Leone to fetch a passel of slaves, and being as how neither you nor Boko and I relish the idea of spending all that gold to buy those slaves, it might not be a bad idea to use the frigate's cargo for our trading purposes. That is, if she is carrying a rich enough cargo.'

'All right,' Juan laughed, 'we shall see what we shall see.'

All that night the *Panther* continued bowling after the frigate through a moonwashed sea like a wolf with froth streaming from its jaws as the craft leaped after her. The next morning both vessels were still skimming the water under every inch of canvas they could spread, reeling over on their sides each time the breezes spanked and freshened against the canvas, slicing through white caps and spray that bubbled and sparkled in the sun, leaving widening tracks of foamy current in their wakes as their bows plunged at times sharply into the waves and out again, flashing up high to the fore-yards, and then seething and washing in froth that rippled around their rudders and was churned under again in the wakes astern.

Weary of the chase, Juan decided to risk losing headway

by putting a couple of eighteens into her backside which was now two cable lengths forward of them. Taking the helm himself, Juan maneuvered the *Panther* until her forward cannon was coming into position. He waited until the precise moment before giving Boko the command to fire. Boko touched the torch to the fuse and the heavy gun barked, sending a round into the frigate's fantail. The crew primed and reloaded and stood by as Juan worked the helm to keep from losing headway as they yawed and swung in the opposite direction. Again he gave the command to fire. The cannon barked and the frigate's mizzen top gallant mast sheared off, sending spar and canvas and line falling to the deck, taking with it the braces and bumpkins.

Taking advantage of the frigate's increasing loss of forward speed, Juan again jockeyed the *Panther*'s bowsprit into position like a wind-driven spear pointing the way. He called for Boko to stand fast, to take aim, then he gave the command to fire. Boko's shot was uncannily accurate. The eighteen pounder ripped a hole in the main top gallant and bounced through the main, rending it useless as the weighty ball tore a gaping hole through the canvas.

Maneuvering the swift *Panther* into position now to blast a hole in the frigate's hull with the thirteen portside guns, Juan picked up the trumpet as the sloop lightly skimmed the sea keeping a constant distance between them and shouted, 'Strike your colors and lay down your arms or we send you to the bottom!'

The captain of the helpless frigate at once ordered the ensign pulled down. He lifted his trumpet and shouted across to Juan, 'Let us continue on our voyage. We'll pay you ten thousand in gold as tribute.'

Gideon's face was glowing when Juan glanced at him. Both men eyed each other for a moment, pleased with their bloodless victory, then Juan shouted through the trumpet again, 'Whither are you bound and what's your cargo?'

'We are the *Lord Dunsmore* bound for Cardiff our home port with a cargo of tobacco and cotton and three passengers. Our cargo is of no value to you since it is too heavy and bulky to be transferred to your vessel in these seas. We beg of you, please accept our offer of gold as tribute.'

'By whose authority do you make an offer of tribute?'

'By none other than Lord Dunsmore, the owner of this ship.'

'Very well,' Juan shouted, 'I shall like to see this Lord Dunsmore. Have him and your passengers brought to the poop.'

There was some scurrying about on the decks of the frigate. The *Panther*, still under full canvas, made a full circle around the vessel and drew along the port side again. Juan gave the wheel to Tubal and went to the starboard rail with trumpet and glass. He saw two men, one a tall be-whiskered man and a portly young man beside him on deck trying to shield from view a young lady wearing a pink frock and ribboned bonnet. Juan fixed his glass on the girl and for a long while he stood as though mesmerized. Never before had he seen such a lovely creature, so pink and soft and rounded and white of skin.

Juan turned aside and nodded to Gideon. 'We'll go aboard. I mean to have that woman for myself. But whatever you do, don't let her see what we shall do to the crew. Is that clear?'

Gideon smiled. 'Shall I tap her on the noggin'?'

'No, just seize her and bring her aboard. Lock her in the chart locker in my cabin. Now pass the word to the men to stand by for boarding. Upon my signal I want every white head aboard that frigate to roll.'

Minutes later the grapples were thrown and the two hulls lashed together. Juan, armed with a pistol and cutlass, led his men aboard the frigate. He strode up to the poop deck where the captain, the mate, the helmsman, and the three passengers were standing and then returned the captain's salute with a curt one of his own. He stepped forward boldly and with pistol and cutlass still in hand, extended his arms. 'Your sword, please, captain.'

The captain hastily unbuckled his sword hanger and gave the ornamental weapon to Juan. Then he said, 'Captain, sir, I see from your manners that you are a gentleman and an officer. Please help yourselves to our money chests and spare our noble passengers and crew.'

Juan turned and stared at the girl. Although she averted her face and tried to conceal herself behind her father, she still could not hide her great beauty from view. At close range she was even lovelier than Juan had imagined. His breath caught in his throat with expectancy as he saw Gideon coming up behind the girl, blade in hand.

Before the frigate's master, passengers, and crew, realized

it, Juan's pirates not only had them surrounded, but as well had their naked blades against the backs and throats. Juan gave Gideon the nod. Gideon moved forward and seized the girl. She screamed and tried to struggle. The men in the crew and on the poop made motions as if to resist but they were stopped by cold steel pressing against their vital parts. Gideon carried the kicking, shrieking girl over his shoulders in one hand as he stepped lightly up to the rail and jumped across to the *Panther.* He carried her into the forward companionway and then down to Juan's cabin where she could still be heard screaming and wailing her futile protests.

Indignant with the outrage of seeing Lord Dunsmore's daughter kidnaped right before their eyes, the captain brazenly stepped forward and shouted in Juan's face, 'You dastardly black heathen, you sea demon! You gave your word there'd be none of this!'

'Whoa, there, mon capitaine!' Juan laughed, nudging the man back with the point of his blade which he twisted playfully in hand. 'I made no promise and I accepted none of your offers.' He laughed and glanced round to make certain the crew aboard the frigate had been disarmed and rendered helpless. Then he said, 'Why should I? When I hold the upper hand and my crew and I have you at our mercy, why should we take a paltry ten thousand in gold when we can have everything?'

At that, the men shouted and moved menacingly toward their prisoners. Suddenly, several pistol shots rent the air just above Juan's head as balls went flying inches from his skull. Juan spun around, dropping the captain's surrendered sword. From the rigging aloft he glimpsed a seaman with two pistols. Juan fired from the shoulder, felling the man with the single shot. The man cried out on his way down. His body struck the capstan with a sickening thud.

Taking advantage of the momentary diversion, the captain quickly whipped up his sword from the deck where Juan had dropped it, slipped the blade out of the scabbard and stepped toward the pirate captain.

Juan laughed and danced back. He tossed away his empty pistol and began parrying the captain's desperate sword thrusts. The frigate captain was no match for the experienced Juan. Several minutes after they had been playing their swords, Juan wearied of the sport and ran the captain through. He withdrew his blade and turned, snatching up the sword which the captain, now breathing his last gurgling breath, had dropped. He tossed the blade to Lord Dunsmore and laughingly said, 'I have a bargain for you, your lordship. Best me with this blade and I'll spare you and your daughter. But let me emerge the victor and I'll spare no one except your daughter whom I shall have as my bride.'

'I'll see my daughter dead before I let a black bastard like you put his hands on her! En garde!'

The lord was remarkably agile for a man his age. An expert swordsman, he drove furiously at Juan, slashing and thrusting right and left with all his strength. The pirate crew relaxed their watchful vigil over the prisoners to look on. As they did so, the men of the crew who had already laid down their arms began to exchange surreptitious glances and all of them looked to several burly fellows who obviously were their petty officers and who had the authority to lead the others in a fight. The white crewmen waited for an opportunity to jump the Negro pirates and that chance arose when Juan's blade drew blood.

With a sudden outcry the white prisoners whirled on their captors and a fierce fight ensued. Juan, seeing what happened during a brief respite in the duel as he jumped up to the watchrail and danced in the air over the lord's slashing blade, decided to make short work of it. He jumped down and took the offensive, driving Lord Dunsmore back to the edge of the rail. He smashed his blade across the lord's sword, and with a deft twist of the wrist, disarmed him. He laughed and paused one brief moment before skewering him in the belly. Withdrawing his blade, Juan spun round and chased the third white man from the poop. The fellow, screaming, clambered up the rail and tried to climb the shrouds but slipped and bumped his head and fell like a sack of lead shot into the churning sea thirty feet below.

Gideon and Boko fought their ways to Juan's side, then the three of them waded down the ladder from the poop into the melee, slashing and killing, like threshers cutting a swath through the body of white crewmen who had somehow managed to arm themselves with sheath knives, cutlasses, clubs and belaying pins. During the ensuing quarter hour the decks of the frigate ran red with blood of her dead and dying crewmen who were no match for the savage pirates whose years of experience with blade and dirk could not be challenged.

When it was all over, fifteen of Juan's crew was left and of these, six were suffering from wounds. Juan suffered a gash in the head and Gideon had received a cut across the cheek. Boko was unscathed.

Not a white man had been spared.

After the bodies of the dead had been tossed to the circling sharks, Juan bound up his head with a scarf and went below with the men to search the vessel. They found the specie which the captain had offered in tribute in addition to several hundred pounds sterling which had been secreted behind a loose board in the bulkhead of the captain's cabin. When this was found the crew began a renewed search for hidden wealth. It was not until all the goods and cargo they could transfer to the *Panther* had been loaded that Boko and several of his men found, concealed in the bilges where tar had been poured, a hundred thousand pieces of eight. At the find which had to be dug out with knives, a handful at a time, the men went mad with excitement. There was no doubt in their minds that Lord Dunsmore had been transferring funds from places of concealment in America to his estate at Dunsmore near their destination of Cardiff. It was indeed the richest haul they had ever made.

It was not until the following morning that all the treasure had been collected together aboard the *Panther* and divided amongst the men. Only after this had been done was the *Lord Dunsmore* sent to the bottom by three well-placed fourteen pound balls at point-blank range.

Bleary-eyed from lack of sleep and the excitement, Juan and the others met in the mess room forward and discussed what they should do next. Since they had so much wealth was there any use in continuing the voyage to Africa to buy a cargo of slaves?

The men voted unanimously to abandon the idea and put about at once for the Port of Havana so they might have a spree for themselves and enjoy a well earned respite from the rigors of the life they had been leading. Juan concurred and a course was set for Havana. Then he went below and unlocked the door to his cabin. He was anxious to make the acquaintance of the noblewoman he had captured and was beginning to develop some rather fanciful ideas about her and their future relationship.

The moment the white girl was released from the locker in which she had been confined for eighteen hours, she rushed at Juan with tooth and nail bared. 'You beast!' she hissed, 'you bloodthirsty black beast! I heard it all – you killed my father and all those innocent men. If it's the last thing I do, if it takes my dying breath, I'll avenge this atrocity!'

Juan, holding her at bay, his big hands gripping both her wrists, stood tall above her, seeing only her pale blue eyes, her flushed cheeks, her soft flawless creamy white skin, the petal soft fullness of her lips, and he knew in that moment that it would be worth everything he possessed, goods, treasure, ship, and everything if he could receive in return the love of this woman. Suddenly he felt a quality of compassion sweep through him he had never before known. Suddenly he wanted to drop to his knees and beg this woman, this girl-woman, to forgive him. But he was Panther John and he could not go to his knees for anyone, man or woman, lord or lady, nobleman, king, or God.

'I did not want the blood of your father and the others on my hands. I did not draw my blade until the captain, and then after I killed him, your father, crossed blades with me. I'm sorry, my lady.'

'Y-you vicious savage, you nigger, you heathen!' she fumed, her eyes flecked with glints of fire, her sharp teeth bared. 'What are you going to do with me?'

'That depends on you.'

She stopped trying to jerk free of his grasp. She sighed and began to weep. Then she sank to her knees on the deck and as Juan released her, she covered her face with her hands.

Totally moved by her pathetic grief, Juan stood helplessly beside the chart table looking down at her. He wanted to speak, to tell her what was in his heart, that he was not the murderer and blackguard she thought he was; that he was different from all the others, but he could never utter such words to her for these were utterances Panther John the pirate could never humble himself to make. Not if he lived forever would he learn to admit such things.

'My lady,' he said finally when he had wearied of standing by and watching her crumpled figure on the deck as she lay weeping, 'we will talk later when you have recovered from your grief. In the meantime, you will be quartered in this cabin.' He went to the door and opened it to reveal a small compartment with bed, chair, and lantern. Above the chair was a small barred window through which shimmers of sunlight reflecting upon the surface of the sea danced upon the overhead beams.

'Come Maria,' he said, 'go quietly or else I shall drag you.'

She looked up at his face before she arose and asked, 'How did you learn my name?'

Juan smiled. He turned and pointed at several large trunks which had been placed just inside the door of the adjoining cabin. 'Aren't those your belongings?'

'Yes.'

'And is that not your name painted on each trunk?'

Maria Dunsmore stood up. She wiped the streaks of tears from her cheeks and then, holding her head proudly erect, marched into the cabin and pulled the door shut after her. Juan heard her slide the bolt into place. He smiled, turned the key in the lock, and then went to his bunk where he dropped wearily down upon his back. He crossed his legs and rested his boots on the footboard. Exhausted as he was, he did not drop off to sleep for he could not sleep. His mind was filled with thoughts of his future and what he would do next, once they reached Havana. He toyed with the idea of buying a sugar plantation and settling down to a peaceful life as a planter, and he considered the idea of going to a big city in Europe where he would live like a prince in a fine townhouse with servants to wait on him; but then he liked better the idea of winning Maria Dunsmore's hand in marriage. He did not consider the problems which would arise if such a thing ever did happen – all that mattered to Juan was the thought that it *could* happen and that would please him more than anything else in the world.

HAVANA, CUBA
June 21, 1821
Thursday
8 p.m.

Except for Juan, Boko, the captive white girl, Maria Dunsmore, and the two crewmen who had been unfortunate enough to draw the short straws for the first watch as gangplank sideboys, the *Panther* was deserted, riding at her moorings against the Malecon quay of Havana harbor.

Boko, who was in no particular haste to go ashore and spend his share of the money, sat on deck forward of the main, swigging from a jug of rum. He was perfectly content to sit quietly, watching the lights of Havana, humming to himself and musing over what he would do with all that money. Before the others had left the vessel in a mad rush to celebrate their good fortune by whooping it up in the bordellos and taverns of the city, Boko had vainly tried to reason with them, to dissuade them from being unwise and dissipating the small fortunes each man now possessed. He had failed in his efforts and had nearly been bowled over when the men dashed for the gangplank as soon as the lines were secured.

Although he had no idea whatsoever what he would do with such a sum as he now had, Boko was not to perturbed, for he had long since learned it was far wiser to save one's money than it was to spend it without thought or reason. It was the simple things in life which had always been Boko's prime source of joy; he was content just to be comfortable with a full belly and a jug of rum or wine; he was content to sit alone contemplating the world around him; and most of all he was content to sit back and watch his prophecies come true. While it was also true that many of his predictions were incorrect and frequently did not materialize as he had prophesied, it was likewise true that an uncanny number *had* come true exactly as he had said they would; precisely as he had so clearly seen them in the ashes he read.

Now that the crew was ashore in Havana, and now that Juan was below in his cabin – with his prisoner – Boko was sitting back against the mainmast almost totally intoxicated. He would have drunk himself into a stupor had it not been for his curiosity about something he had predicted, but had not told anyone he had foreseen would happen that every evening. To be sure, Boko wanted to be sober enough to observe his prediction coming true.

Somewhere in the city the chimes of a cathedral tolled the hour. In the distance he heard the sound of trotting horses pulling carts and coaches. Overhead, wheeling high above upon the thermals below the darkening sky, a man-o-war bird hung motionless as if awaiting too that which Boko had prophesied would occur that night.

Juan, in his cabin at the writing desk, lit the lanterns which swung from the overhead upon wrought-iron chains, and went to Maria's locked door. After listening a moment, he tapped lightly.

'What is it this time?'

'Come out, Maria. Be civil and we'll get on together.'

'I don't wish to get on with you. I want to be free. I want you to let me go. This port, is it a city? I thought I heard church bells, but I don't know. We're moored, aren't we?' Then, after a long pause, the sound of the bolt sliding open was heard. The door opened and Maria, attired in a long white embroidered dress with hoop skirts and a black shawl, stood framed in the doorway. She stood gazing at Juan for several minutes before she slowly moved into the center of the cabin. Then she bolted for the open windows and started over the cushioned seat as if to throw herself into the sea.

Juan caught her by the ankle and roughly pulled her down to the cushions. He laughed and said, 'If you want to go ashore and see the sights of Havana, all you need do is be civil to me.'

She glared at him, her eyes spitting blue flame reflected from the lanterns. '*Never!*' she cried. 'I'd rather die first. You know what you are – you're a – '

'Don't say that again!' Juan commanded, his face hardening into a brown mask of contempt. 'I apologize for not being of noble birth; but I do not apologize for who I am or what I am or what I have done. I, however,' he said, suddenly smiling and standing up, releasing her, bowing from the waist, 'forgive *you* for being my unwilling guest. Now if you are willing – '

'Go to hell, you – you Satan!'

Hands on his hips, Juan tilted his head back and roared with laughter. Before he could think of another thing to say suddenly the cabin door burst open and three Negroes with drawn knives and pistol rushed into the room. Juan turned and recognized them as being three of the men who had been left ashore in Havana the month before when they started out on the journey for Africa.

'You was a fool for coming back to Havana, cap'n. Didn't you know we'd be watching and waiting?'

Juan made no move. He offered no reply. He stood fast, watching the trio through slitted eyes.

'Aye, cap'n, we was waiting and watching. We knowed you would be putting in soon, but not this soon. You double-crossed us and we're here for our share.'

'What are you talking about?' Juan asked.

'We mean the booty you divided with the men who you didn't abandon here in Havana.'

'Yeah, cap'n, how about our share? And yours too.'

Juan smiled. 'I still don't understand what you're driving at. After we left you we took a prize and came back to pick you men up. What else is there to say?'

Two of the men looked toward the white girl. The younger of the trio went toward her and suddenly, unexpectedly, seized her dress by the neckline and ripped it off her body. Maria screamed. Juan made a move as if to stop him but two blades pressing against his throat halted him.

'A right spunky hellcat, h'ain't she?' the one who had stripped Maria laughed. 'I think I'll lower my anchor into her bottom.'

'No, wait!' Juan said, moving again to stop him, unmindful of the razor sharp blades pressing against his throat. 'Let the white woman alone. I'm holding her for ransom. If she's harmed we all will have hell to pay. She's the daughter of some nobleman.'

'Yeah?' the man said, leering at Juan. 'How much ransom money is yo' asking, Panther John?'

Juan clenched his fists in helpless frustration. He exhaled and replied, 'Fifty thousand pesos. Gold.'

The men raised their eyebrows and exchanged glances. Then one of the two holding the blades against his throat said, 'Being as how she's worth thet much to a Englishman she oughter be worth trice fifty thousand. Unless you don't want to see us pleasure ourselfs with her and slice her into fish bait, suppose you make it worth our while to spare her. How about it, Panther John?'

Juan glared at them, then looked toward Maria. She was cringing in a corner beside the table holding the tatters of her garments over her bosom and crotch. In the lantern light her pale white flesh was the hue of ripe peach. During that moment Juan knew he would never forgive himself unless he did what he was about to do. He drew a deep breath and looked at the three men. 'All right, you win. My gold in exchange for the girl's life.'

'How 'bout Boko and them other two chaps topside?' one man reminded the others.

'Yup, forgot 'bout them. The two sideboys we throw in free. But Boko – he is costsome. For your life, the girl's, and Boko's, all the specie and gold you got aboard. Is thet a bargain, Panther John?'

'Do I have any say in the matter?'

'Wal, maybe you would've if you didn't of dumped us all all in Havana like you did. The rest of the crew warn't so smart as we all is. They joined up with another pirate crew out of the Isle of Pines. But us, we hanged around waiting on you to come back like we knowed you was bounden to do.'

'Very well, so you're all very clever.'

'Where is it, Panther John?' the second man with the blade against his throat demanded, accenting his words with the point of his sharp weapon.

'Aboard is almost one hundred seventy-five thousand pesos worth of gold, silver, Spanish Joes, and pieces of eight. Before I tell you where it's hid, I want you to put the girl, Boko, and the two crewmen ashore with me.'

'Nuthin' doin', Panther John,' one man nodded emphatically. 'You all stay aboard right here in this cabin until we helps ourselfs and get away.'

'That's fair,' Juan said. 'Now go fetch Boko and the others and lock us in – then I'll tell you.'

'You sure h'ain't a trusting soul, is yo'?'

Juan showed his teeth in what was supposed to be a smile. It was a stalemate for the moment, but he knew he was holding the upper hand: the gold.

'Quit tawking and get Boko and them other two niggers and bring 'em down heah!'

The younger of the trio hurried out and went up the ladder two rungs at a time. Several minutes later he returned, herding before him, the two sideboys who were half-carrying, half-dragging Boko.

When Juan saw Boko stumbling down the companionway he gave an angry start but was stopped by the blades pressing into his throat. 'He ain't hurt none. He is jest drunk.'

As soon as Boko stumbled into the cabin, Juan relaxed. Then the trio backed away toward the door, their pistols leveled at Juan and the girl. 'All right, where is it?'

Juan stood his ground. 'I'm not telling you until that door is closed and bolted from this side and you cutthroats are outside.'

'Thet's your word as a cap'n?'

Juan nodded.

The trio held a whispered conference. One of the three backed out of the cabin and was heard running topside. His bootsteps crossed the deck above and then stopped at the watchrail below which was the cabin window. The men grinned at Juan knowingly as they said, by way of a rejoiner to his unuttered thoughts, 'Thet's in case you're thinking of getting tricky.'

At this, they backed out of the cabin and closed the door. Juan moved quickly across the deck and dropped the heavy iron into place, securely locking them in. Then he shouted through the door, 'Tween decks just aft of the foremast you'll find a nail driven into one of the sister ribs. Attached to that nail is a line. Pull that line up and you'll find it's tied to a braided hemp rope. Pull it and you'll find hanging from it, down inside the hull between the planks and the hull, eight heavy gunny sacks. The specie and bullion are in those sacks.'

'Watch thet door if they might be trying a trick,' one man said. 'I'll go look. Whistle if'n they tries any sly moves.'

Juan looked at the two seamen and then at Maria. She had sidled to the door leading into her tiny cabin, still holding the ragged garment to cover her nakedness. She gave him a look of entreaty. Juan averted his eyes discreetly and nodded, giving her permission to retire and make herself decent. She slipped through the door in a wink and closed it after her softly.

Boko, sober enough to realize what was happening, but too drunk to stand, dropped heavily to a wooden arm chair and cocked his rotund head in an attempt to focus his vision on Juan. He clucked his tongue noisily and nodded. 'Sech a danged shame, losing all thet treasure t'scurvy rats like them thar.'

Juan said nothing. He went to the small liqueur chest above his desk and took down a decanter and three small dram glasses. He placed the glasses on the desk and poured a thimbleful into each. Then he gave a glass to the two crewmen and grinned at Boko who he had deliberately not provided a glass.

'I know'n h'it, I done drunk me fill awready.'

The men laughed as they received a nod from Juan and helped themselves. Juan toasted them and said, 'Easy come, easy go.'

Everyone laughed and tossed down the liqueur, a fine French aperitif with an aromatic bouquet. As Juan stood contemplating his empty glass, shouts and footsteps were heard approaching. The gold had been found. But the brigands did not dare leave Juan's cabin door unguarded. They had sailed under him for too many years to trust him or his word and they knew full well Juan had not given his word.

Muffled voices were heard as the trio discussed their plans to take the gold and flee. Then footsteps were heard approaching the cabin door. The sound of tools clinking was heard next. And then a hammer driving a nail into the door jamb to secure them inside, leaving only one way out, through the windows above the fantail of the vessel.

The hammering ceased after six nails had been driven completely through the door and the jamb into which it was fitted. Juan put down his glass and went to the door. He nodded with displeasure and said, 'I feel worse about them ruining my fine woodwork than I do about losing the money to them.'

Several minutes later footsteps were heard clunking across the deck overhead toward the gangway, coming from the number two companionway through which the Negroes had emerged carrying their weighty burden. Juan and the others listened intently until they heard the footsteps reach the stones of the quay. Then Juan reached under his bunk and drew out a polished walnut case. He opened the brass fitting which locked it and withdrew two duelling pistols. He shoved one in his belt and carrying the other in his right hand, he stepped onto the cushions before the aft windows and stepped out on the transom. As he emerged and clung to the carved brightwork trim he caught a glimpse of the trio hurrying up the stone steps leading to the Malecon where a horse and carriage stood waiting. He momentarily lost sight of them as they came up behind the stone wall. Then he pulled himself up to the polished quarterdeck rail and stepped over, He stood fast and drew the second pistol. Holding both weapons in his fists, Juan braced them upon the rail and stood waiting for the men to show themselves as they came into view at the side of the open carriage door. The moment they reached the carriage and began to heave their heavy sacks inside, Juan aimed and squeezed the triggers. One man screamed and jerked upright, falling backward, both hands clutching the back of his head. The second man lurched to one side, but managed to keep his balance. He dove into the carriage and hurriedly dragged inside the last sack. The third man, crouching behind the Malecon wall, drew his pistol and stood waiting and watching for Juan to show himself. Juan could not do so because he knew the crewman to be an expert shot. Moreover, his weapons were empty and there was nothing he could do further.

The man crouching behind the wall backed to his feet and moved cautiously toward the carriage. In the rapidly fading daylight he could still distinguish anyone moving on deck twenty-five yards away and at that range Juan knew such a marksman would not miss.

He cursed his luck and remained in the shadows, watching helplessly as the man climbed into the driver's seat and picked up the reins in one hand. Then with a lurch the carriage began to draw away from the quayside, the horse's hooves clattering on the time-worn cobblestones.

Juan jumped to the deck and ran down the gangplank, hurling his useless weapons into the green sea, cursing at the top of his voice in disgust. He raced along the quay and then up the stone steps to the Malecon promenade above, arriving in time to see the carriage speeding around a corner and disappearing in the gloom of early evening blanketing La Habana.

When he returned to the vessel the two crewmen had forced the cabin door open and were removing the nails from the woodwork with a claw hook. Juan frowned at the damage and then opened the door to the ship's armory with the great key he wore around his neck. He broke out pistols and muskets and handed them to the men. 'One of you go aloft and see that no one else boards us who ain't in our crew. And you,' Juan said, turning to the second man, 'challenge anyone who even approaches the ship along the quay. I don't care who goes aloft first, just hop to it. But first, take Boko to his cabin and put him to bed.'

The men put the weapons in their belts and hastened to carry out Juan's orders, struggling with Boko's dead weight in an attempt to get him to walk out of the cabin. It was useless. They had to carry him, one man at his feet, the other behind his shoulders. Juan moved to the door and held it ajar as they went out. Then he closed the door after them and returned to the liqueur decanter. He poured himself another drink and as he stood sipping from the glass, he heard the rustle of skirts behind him. He turned and saw Maria Dunsmore entering the cabin from her cubicle. She halted, tiny hands clasped before her, head bowed. Without elevating her gaze she said, staring down at the deck planks, 'I don't quite know what to say.'

'Concerning what?'

She slowly lifted her face. She was biting her bottom lip as she fixed her gaze on him. 'Concerning what you just did. I never expected that you would make such a great sacrifice like that – for me. I rather thought you would let them rape me and while they were doing that, you would attack and overpower them.'

Juan took another glass from the chest and placed it upon the desk. He uncorked the glass stopper of the decanter and slowly poured a drink, then refilled his own glass. He lifted both glasses and extended one to her. She hesitated a moment, then stepped forward, bowing her head, averting her eyes as she accepted the glass.

Before she raised it to her lips she stood uneasily, as though trying to say something else she had on her mind. Juan remained silent, studying her, waiting, intent on her every movement. During the time she had been his captive this was the first time she showed any civility toward him.

'Captain Panther John,' she said rather stiffly, still avoiding his probing eyes, 'I want to thank you, and ask if you meant that, about holding me for ransom.' She lifted her gaze to his and asked, 'Are you holding me for ransom?'

Juan smiled. 'No.'

'Then you only said that in order to trick them into letting me alone?'

He nodded.

'Then *why* are you still keeping me locked up?'

Juan swallowed hard. He eyed her and shrugged. From the expression on his face and the manner in which he stood, the white girl grasped something of the thoughts in Juan's mind.

'What will you do with me?'

'That's for me to decide. I have a large investment in you now. I could buy two hundred slaves for what I just lost on your account.'

'I expect you could.'

Juan lifted his glass and toasted her with a warm smile and words: 'The great virtue of her/Doth fill me with wonder; Her beauteous countenance/My poor soul doth entrance; And though it stops my breath, Is like a glimpse of death, Her beauty exquisite/Is my life's requisite.'

Maria's mouth opened with a slight gasp of pleasant surprise. 'Panther John, you are a most remarkable person. I hardly expected you to know Clément Marot.'

'You know the lines?'

She blushed and dipped her chin. Then she recited: 'Ye who would wish delight /From no more than the sight/Of beauty and of grace, And ye who would efface/A thousand ills will see /The other part of me, She who is my mistress, Whom God doth keep and bless.'

Juan blinked and smiled. The chance recall of those lines from the slim leather bound book he had so often perused in Gaspar's cabin when he had been a boy-slave had now said for him that which he had been unable to express for he could not humble himself before this woman.

As soon as she had recanted the lines, Maria's cheek turned a deep purple as the realization of the poem's meaning became clear to her. Quick to change the subject of conversation, Maria downed her drink and turned round with a rustling of her petticoats. She then asked, without looking in Juan's direction, 'What will you do now?

'Yes, *now* that you have been robbed and you are penniless.'

'Who said I'm penniless?'

She turned and peered sidewise at him, amusement crinkling her eyes, disbelief in her tone. 'Don't tell me you have more money aboard this vessel?'

'Not aboard, but buried back at Panther Cay there is a chest I'd nearly forgotten.'

'Do you intend going to this – this Panther Cay to get it?'

'Perhaps someday I might.'

'And until then?'

'We've a long voyage to make – across the Atlantic Sea to Sierra Leone.'

'Sierra Leone?' she frowned. 'Isn't that the slave coast?'

'Yes.'

'You are a slaver – among other things?'

Juan wearied of the banter. He had told her far too much already. He went to the cabin door and locked it and then hung the key around his neck. Then he went to the window seat and sat down. He removed his boots and then shrugged out of his coat. As he began to take off his silk shirt, Maria found her voice and asked in a shocked whisper, 'What are you doing?'

'Going to bed.'

'There? Your bunk's over there.'

Juan smiled. He fired a glance toward the windows and then looked at her. 'The only way out is through there. You'll have to climb over me if you try that – and I might as well tell you, I'm a light sleeper.'

'Oh, you!' she said with a haughty sniff, turning in fury and sweeping out of the cabin with her hooped skirts rocking to and fro as she entered her tiny compartment and slammed the door after her.

Juan, chuckling, turned on his side upon the window seat cushions, pulled his jacket over his face, folded his arms, and closed his eyes.

THE VILLAGE OF TOSA MAJINA,
SIERRA LEONE COUNTRY, AFRICA
July 29, 1821
Sunday
3 a.m.

Juan, Boko, Gideon, and the ten crewmen who had not jumped ship in Havana six weeks before, stood on deck watching in grim silence as the grotesque figures of the Negro slaves trudged up the sloping gangway after climbing out of the native boats which had brought them out to the ship. Juan and his crew had purchased one hundred seventy-seven prime men and women from Chief M'gumog of the village of Tosa Majina. But it had been Boko who had made the initial contact with the chief on the previous evening after they had dropped anchor off the Sierra Leone river basin. After the initial palaver, the chief who was highly gratified to do business with men of his race, invited them to spend a few hours in his harem, and then, after the orgiastic interlude had been concluded, they were taken to the heavily guarded barracoon, the walled enclosure in which the slaves awaiting sale to traders were imprisoned. When the price was agreed upon for a lot which Boko and Gideon personally inspected by manipulating limbs and muscles, examining joints, armpits, mouths, teeth, breasts, buttocks, and groins, in that order without regard to sex, but with close attention paid to agility, soundness of chest and back, firmness of breast, clearness of eye, and lack of deformity, it was also agreed that the coffles would be delivered to the vessel early enough for departure on the five a.m. tide.

This done, the packing cases and barrels on the decks of the *Panther* were promptly transferred to the native boats who returned on each trip with twenty-five slaves. When the final count was tallied, and one hundred sixteen males ranging in age from ten to twenty-three were placed in the forward hold beneath the forecastle, and the sixty-one girls and women were quartered between decks, Juan and the chief sat upon the deck sorting into even stacks the gold specie they had agreed upon.

Before the robbery, Juan had secreted beneath a tightly fitted plank in the deck below the table in his cabin a large leather bag containing seventeen thousand dollars in American gold coins of all denominations. It was this nest egg which Juan had used to negotiate the purchase. When the counting was done and additional *bugnee* gifts were given the chief to sweeten the deal, the chief embraced Juan, Boko, and Gideon, and then departed with his garishly attired aides in bright paint, animal skins, and feather headdress, beating drums heralding their leave-taking aboard native outriggers.

Shortly before five o'clock the crew went to their stations all except Boko and Gideon who went to see to the slaves to make sure they understood what would happen if they did not obey their orders. Boko, who could speak the several *patois* of the slaves, made it quite clear that Panther John, a black man like themselves was their master and he had decreed none would be chained provided they cooperated and did not make noise or trouble.

Boko also told them fanciful stories about how they would be well treated and taken to a new land where they would only be enslaved for a short time before being set free. The Negroes understood enough of Boko's palaver to ask questions. Boko silenced them by ordering them not to speak unless they were first spoken to. Then he smiled and with wild gestures, told them he had once been a slave, but had been set free by the master of the vessel, Panther John, the messiah.

At this, the natives began singing a chant in praise of Juan, and everything was under control. Topside, Juan was shouting commands to the crew. He was annoyed by the chanting from below, but he did not let that bother him. He picked up the trumpet and bellowed through it at the men.

'Reefers, climb aloft, pronto, pronto! You there, up to the fore. And you and you. Trip aloft to the main and mizzen tops and look sharp there. Stand by the anchor – all hands up anchor! In with the capstan bars, clamp them nippers! Step lively, my buckos! We've a cargo of black ivory aboard that'll make us rich!'

'Anchor's under foot, sar!' sang out the crew forward.

'Very well, then. Pawl the capstan! Sail-loosers, aloft! Trice up. Lay out. Now loose away!' Almost at the very instant his command was given, Gideon appeared on deck and shouted up, 'All ready with the fore – the main – the mizzen. Let fall! Sheets home! Hoist away the tops'ls!'

'You there, cat the anchor and skip aloft to the fors'l gang.'

In response to the terse commands of the captain and his first officer, the *Panther*, under billowing clouds of spanking canvas began to move westward.

By the time the sun appeared over the rapidly disappearing landfall astern, the lookouts had been stationed aloft on the first watch with instructions to keep a sharp eye out for British and American men o'war, and Boko was supervising the feeding and toilette of the slaves billeted in the forward section.

Juan turned the helm over to Tubal and went to see how Boko was managing. He nodded in approval at the troughs of salt water which had been placed on deck for the slaves' use; and he also approved the kitchen arrangement which enabled seventy slaves at each sitting to eat on deck in the fresh air and do some brief, vigorous exercise. With that considerate method of treating the slaves, Juan was confident they would not lose any of them due to ill health or poor morale during the middle passage. He had seen slavers first hand, as had Boko, Gideon, and the others, and he wanted none of that kind of mistreatment aboard the *Panther*.

Shortly before sundown that first day at sea, Juan stood at the taffrail beside Boko and Gideon, idly discussing their plans.

Boko, who had kept close tabs on their investment, rubbed his palms together briskly, almost greedily, as he reported their total investment was sixteen thousand dollars, which meant they had purchased them per head at one hundred eleven dollars American money. 'If'n we puts in at New Orleans or Natchez, we oughter fetch us no less'n a thousand a head. Prime niggers sech as these here is in demand.'

Juan frowned and looked at Gideon. 'What do you think?'

'Natchez, of course. The Havana market is off. Best we can hope for is four, maybe five hunnert a head there. But if we smuggle them up to Natchez, we'll be richer by a hundred and sixty thousand dollars.'

'What yo' mean, a hunnert and sixty? H'it's a hunnert and sixty-one by my calculation.'

Gideon nodded. 'You're wrong, Boko. It costs us a thousand to feed them, don't it?'

Boko allowed that. Then the argument began concerning the division of the spoils. Gideon wanted Juan and Boko and his own share to total fifty thousand dollars each. This left twenty-two hundred dollars apiece for each of the crew. He summed up his argument by winking and saying, 'If we pay them off in gold and silver coin, of small denominations, it'll seem like a fortune to them. I'm all for keeping the lion's share to ourselves. I see no reason for letting those deck monkeys know the score, do you?'

Juan eyed Boko nod approvingly. Then he shrugged and moved away from the rail. 'Consider it done, gents.'

As Juan started for his cabin, Gideon went over to him and inquired, 'How are you and her ladyship getting on? Make any headway with her yet?'

Juan halted and after a moment of hesitation, shrugged. 'Not yet. But mark my words, she'll come crawling to me before this voyage is up.'

Gideon was highly amused. He shook his head in disgust and said, 'If it was me, I would strip her naked and pleasure the hell out of her. Them dandified noble ladies of her breeding ain't no different from woolly-headed wenches, the coal black ones or yaller ones, they're all the same.'

Juan squinted at Gideon and stubbornly nodded. 'No, either she comes to me of her own free will or I won't have her at all. If it's a stupid goddamn wench I want, that's one thing. But I love this white woman.'

Gideon sighed. He was as wise and discerning as he was experienced in the fifty years of living he had lived, loved, fought through, and survived. 'My dear boy,' Gideon said, his arm going around Juan's shoulders, 'Will you stop this ridiculous self delusion and come to your senses? You're a black man and she's a white lady. Get that through your thick skull. It ain't nature for a white lady to come to a black man like she would come to a white man. You read too many books. Your head is filled with too many white men's notions. Think about that, will you? Think about who you are and what you are. You're a pirate and now, a slaver. You're the murderer of her father – '

'I didn't murder Lord Dunsmore. He asked for it and he was the one who tried to do me in first.'

'Makes no difference. From her side of the bed she'll always see you as the black bastard who murdered her father. Can't you get *that* into that woolly head of your'n?'

Juan chewed his lip and earnestly tried to fathom what his lifelong friend, teacher, and confidant was trying to say. For the life of him, he could not abandon the idea of waiting or trying to make Maria Dunsmore voluntarily fall in love with him. But before he thought of a rebuttal, Gideon took his arm and led him to the starboard rail where they would be out of earshot of the other's on deck.

'Look here, Juan,' Gideon said with a watery eye fixed upon him. 'I look upon you as a man looks upon his own flesh and blood kin. We've been through hell together and we've spent some hellish days and nights together, before we got up nerve enough to go up against Gaspar and escape from him, and later when we was on our own, supposedly with a letter of marque, and supposedly members of the pirate brotherhood. Remember those days? Of course you do. And I'm sure you haven't forgotten the day you found out the brotherhood taboo to black men like ourselfs – and that Lafitte was only using us to further his own ends? Am I right?'

Juan allowed that he was with a vacant stare and a nod.

'Sure I'm right, Juan my boy. You know damn well how much I'm right. By the same reasoning am I not right and are you not wrong about that white woman below in your cabin? What do you think she's thinking about you now that you've turned to slave trading and now that you've turned this ship into a goddamn stinking slaver?'

Juan stubbornly pushed Gideon's arm aside. He squared his shoulders and confronted Gideon eye to eye. 'Tell me, old friend, have you ever been in love with a woman?'

Gideon laughed. With a toss of his graying head, he said, 'A hundred, no, a thousand times!'

Juan smiled. It was an unamused smile and there was a touch of sadness in his voice when next he spoke. 'Since I loved – and lost Maha, my life was empty, a void, a nothing. I didn't find another woman to replace her, you know that. Oh, sure, you arranged me to have others, lots of them. But they were just for pleasure, not for love – real honest to God love. Then, that day when I first saw Maria standing on her father's ship, that was the day when I came alive inside all over again. Can you understand that? Can you understand how it feels to want someone so badly you don't even mind losing a king's ransom just to preserve and protect and probably, win her hand?'

'Of course I understand that,' Gideon said. 'Don't forget, my boy, *I* was the one who taught you to read; *I* was the one who smuggled Gaspar's books in for you to read; and *I* was the one who also reminded you that those were white man's writings in white man's books in a white man's world. *I* taught you that a black man don't fall for that sort of romantic gibberish, didn't I?'

Juan nodded. 'Yes, that you did.'

'Let's face it, Juan. When it comes right down to facts, what has that white woman got that any one of those sixty wenches we got aboard don't have, except maybe an education and a white skin? Naked, they all look alike, especially when a man's got a stiff cock.'

'I agree with all you say,' Juan said. 'But you still can't explain why I happen to be in love with that white woman, nor can you tell me *how* I can stop wanting her or how to get her out of my blood.'

Gideon smiled knowingly. A gleam was in his eye as he said, 'Juan, my lad. I'll tell you exactly how to get her out of your blood – one way or the other – this very night if you wish.'

'I'm listening.'

Gideon pursed his lips. He assumed an authoritative manner and pointed at the deck. 'You go right down to your cabin, take out the Bible and exercise your authority as master of this ship.'

'What the hell are you talking about?'

With a sigh of impatience, Gideon explained: 'Don't you get it? Marry up with her. Marry yourself to her. Then, after you have her hand in holy wedlock; after you've wedded her, take her to bed, tear off her clothes, bust her cherry, and pleasure the hell out of her. Tomorrow morning when she wakes up in your bed beside you, either she'll spit in your face or else she'll hold your hand and kiss you. One way or the other it will be. What have you got to lose?'

Juan nodded in agreement. The more he thought about what Gideon had just said, the better he liked the idea. Perhaps Gideon was right; perhaps that was the only way after all with which to deal with Maria Dunsmore. He began to walk towards his cabin, his shoulders snapping back, his head held high, his step quick and now with a purpose.

The moment he unlocked his cabin door and entered, Maria confronted him, hands on her hips, eyes blazing. 'You are worse than Satan!' she shrieked. 'You're a cruel, selfish, inhuman monster.'

'What's this all about?' Juan asked, more amused than he was perturbed or annoyed by her defiant tongue-lashing.

'You know perfectly well what I'm talking about. You, and your poetry – why, you're nothing but a – a Pharaoh, a cruel, cruel persecutor of slaves – a slaver! You're a dirty, evil man. Only a beast would buy and sell other human beings.'

'What are you saying?'

Adamant, her nose held high, Maria spun around the room, skirts swishing, her anger at a fever pitch. 'How could you do such a thing?' she cried finally. 'Buy and sell your own color flesh!'

Juan blinked and asked her, 'How could your father amass such a fortune as he had without slaves to work his cotton and tobacco fields?'

'That was different! Daddy's plantation servants weren't chained and flogged. They weren't mistreated and – '

'Did you see or hear me or my men flogging or chaining or mistreating the slaves aboard this ship?'

'Well, not exactly, but this is different.'

'How so?' Juan demanded. 'Did your father *buy* his slaves?'

'Of course he bought them. Mostly because he didn't want them to be hurt by cruel masters. He kind of liberated them, that's what he did. He cared for them, nursed them when they were sick, fed them, clothed them, gave them nice little houses, and lots of love and kindness.'

Juan laughed. 'Did you see the slaves being brought aboard?'

'Yes. I watched the sight from the windows. It was horrible.'

'What was horrible?'

'The way they were herded together in those outrigger boats like – like cattle. I saw those cruel looking cannibals who brought them. They were the ugliest savages I've ever seen.'

'They were the ones who captured the people I bought.'

'I know that,' she said, pacing the floor angrily, glaring at him, tossing her long tresses each time she cocked an askance eye of accusation at him.

'How would you like being cooped up in one of those savages' barracoons?'

'What's that?'

'The native slave-pens.'

'It would be terrible. Just terrible.'

'Well then, what's so awful about what I've done?'

She frowned, unable to grasp for the moment the point he was making.

'Can't you say that I'm more like Moses instead of Pharaoh?'

'You're a madman!'

'Quite the contrary,' he smiled patiently. 'I rescued them from those cannibals and now I'm delivering them to the promised land just like Moses delivered the children of Israel.'

Openmouthed in astonishment, Maria stopped her pacing and stared at him. She hadn't thought of it that way. She recovered her wit a moment later and with suspicion in her tone, cocked her head at him and inquired, 'Where are you taking those people?'

Juan replied in an off-hand, matter-of-fact tone. 'They'll be given homes on the plantations of some right kindly genteel folks. Where else would I be transporting them?'

'To the slave market, that's where!'

Juan laughed. He walked toward her and grasped her by the hand. She tried to pull away but he held her fast as he peered at her fingers.

'Let me go!'

Juan released her and went to his desk. He opened a small brass box with a key he removed from one of the drawers. He fingered through an assortment of rings and jewelry for several moments and then came toward her holding a gold ring in his hand. He extended it and said, 'Put this on your finger.'

Without asking why, she picked up the ring and slipped it over her ring finger. Juan smiled and turned to the shelf above the liqueur chest. He felt around behind the molding and produced a book which had been behind several folded charts. It was the Holy Bible.

'Come and stand beside me, Maria,' Juan said, grabbing her arm and holding her fast. 'We're going to be married.'

Shock and astonishment registered on her face. She was speechless as she stood there. Unable to speak, laugh, or weep, Maria blinked and gaped up at him.

Unperturbed, Juan took her hand and placed it upon the Bible under his own. Then he said, 'By the grace of the Lord who has invested in me the right to join together a man and a woman in holy matrimony because I am the captain and master of this ship, I hereby take this woman to be my lawful wedded wife until death do us part and I now pronounce Captain Juan Gomez, otherwise known as Panther John, and this white lady, Maria Dunsmore, husband and wife until death us do part. With that ring she just put on her finger, I thee wed up with her.'

'Is this some kind of a joke?' she cried, struggling to break away.

'No, Maria,' Juan said. 'Now that the ceremony is over we're husband and wife. Your friends can call you Mrs Captain Juan Gomez or Mrs Panther John, whichever you prefer.'

'You're insane!' she screamed, clawing his hand until he released her, then backing away from him, screaming, shrinking away in a near-panic.

'No, I'm not insane. I'm your husband now. Scream all you like. Won't do you any good.' With that, Juan stepped toward her, seized her by the front of the dress, and with one violent jerk, stripped it from her body.

Struggling, kicking, clawing at him with tooth and fingernail, Maria fought like a tigress. Juan calmly proceeded to stalk her until she was backed into a corner. He reached for the bodice she was wearing and tore it from her, stripping her nude. Then he put his hands upon her soft rounded hips, ignoring her pounding fists and kicking feet, and carried her to the bed. He dropped her without ceremony and then began to remove his waistcoat, his shirt, his boots, and finally, his pantaloons. At the sight of his hard, lean brown body naked in the lantern light before her, Maria began to tremble visibly as she recoiled on the bed, trying vainly to conceal her own nudity from him.

Juan eyed her soft whiteness and said in a gentle voice, 'Ain't no use fighting me any more. These past weeks I've loved you and wanted you and today I done it – I married you. Now it's my legal right to go to bed with you.'

Paralyzed with fear, Maria could do nothing except stare up at him. No longer fighting, she held herself rigid in a kind of passive resistance as he knelt upon the bed and began to stroke her body with his big brown hands. She held her elbows together, protecting her unkissed breasts. He grasped her wrists and pushed her arms aside to hold her pinned to the mattress. Then he lowered his mouth to her throat, and gently, tenderly, kissed her, breathing deep the sweet scent of her flesh. After a long while he moved up and covered her tiny mouth with his own, forcing her lips to part by thrusting his tongue between them and into her mouth. She neither responded nor struggled. She had given up and now lay quiet and still.

Juan whispered in her hair as he stroked her head and ran his fingers through her tresses, 'I love you, Maria. I loved you from the first moment I saw you.'

'And I loathe you,' she said woodenly. 'You murderer. You Satan. You killed my father in cold blood. I wish you were dead. And after you're done with me, I'll wish I was dead too.'

Undaunted, Juan bent his lips to her rounded breasts. He savored them, licking the pink teats until they grew rigid and the flesh puckered. He stroked her sides and her hips and continued to love her with his mouth and tongue, tasting the fragrance of her soft femininity, breathing deep the heady smell of her.

He moved down and rubbed his beard against the gentle slope of her white belly, gently mouthing her flesh, ever so gently touching his tongue into the depths of her navel. Still, Maria did not respond or move or struggle. She remained entirely passive, but now with eyes closed tight as if seeking to blot the sight of him from her consciousness.

His hands moved beneath her and stroked and kneaded the plump rounds of her buttocks, each big hand nearly covering fully each cheek. He moved lower and pressed his short beard lightly against the blonde down at her groin. He sucked in deep gulps of air through nostrils and mouth, tasting with his senses the slight pungent woman smell of her. Then he began to kiss her thighs, nipping the flesh with his lips, dragging the scraggly ends of his beard along the contours of her perfectly formed rounded limbs. He licked a trail down to each knee and then up again, above the perimeter of soft silk at her groin, and then down over the other thigh. He grasped her legs just above the knees and pressed them apart and back until the knees rested upon her breasts and her parted groin and buttocks were lifted into the air scant inches from his slavering mouth. Slowly, with deliberate lack of haste, Juan brought his lips down until they barely touched the mounds of her womanhood. He placed his tongue lightly, no more than the weight of a feather, upon her moist, pink flesh. He tasted and explored her with his tongue, savoring the virgin flesh that had never before known the tongue or finger or kiss or caress or member of man. He pressed her legs further and further apart and back, lifting her secret cleavages still higher and closer to his mouth. He began to send his tongue spiraling through her parts, flicking over the nodule at the peak of the crevass and whirling downward through the swath of yawning lips to the cheeky rounds of her quivering buttocks and the pink-brown button of her anus. The gentle motion of the ship rocked him in the cradle of her flesh, but still Maria showed no sign of response nor did she protest, resist, or make an outcry.

Juan drew himself up to his knees and moved gracefully between her widespread limbs, his ruddy brown flesh contrasting sharply against her pale whiteness. He clasped her buttocks in his hands and crept closer, his manhood enormous, rigid, throbbing, brown and ruddy tipped, swollen until it was nearly as thick around as her wrist and almost half as lengthy as her forearm.

Unmoving, Maria continued to lay frozen, stiff, silent, her eyes squeezed shut. Juan pretended not to notice, but he was keenly aware of her passivity, her defiant silent resistance.

Now that he had caressed her and loved her, he desired her with a quality of fierce hunger, of robust carnality, of throbbing savagery, and every bone and fibre of his body clamored for the plungings of fulfillment. He steadied himself and cupped her buttocks in his right hand, removing his left only to guide his organ into the right passage. He looked down and saw himself pulsating a hair's breadth from her flesh. Against her virginal smallness it seemed a physical impossibility. He was a giant among men, towering to a height of six feet, six inches, and she was a child-woman with fingers and hands and limbs in miniature of all the other women he had known. Despite this, he felt a sense of craving to cause her pain and anguish, and at the same time to love her and be loved in return. His was not so much a need to possess or love as it was a *need* – a desperate need – to *be* loved. Gripping her tightly, clenching his teeth in order to contain himself, he touched her, aware now of the oozing warmth barely quieting the tip of his manhood. He pressed down and forward and felt his flesh meet her resisting flesh. Of all her being, only her virginity attempted to deny him access. He felt an overpowering sense of surging energy impelling him and he braced himself and drove against her with such might, with such force, it seemed he was trying to bury himself entirely within her. He attained full entry in that fierce bludgeoning onslaught which might have brought bloodcurdling screams of agony and of pain from an ordinary woman – but Maria Dunsmore was no ordinary woman. She did not cry out and she did not resist or give any indication she had pleasure or pain.

When it was over, Juan's sweating body cooled atop hers and he fell asleep with his flesh and his wife's still joined.

It was the sensation of a cool pulsating breeze whipping through the open windows that awakened Juan at dawn the next morning. He opened his eyes and turned to gaze at Maria. She was in the same place and in the same position in which he had left her, only now her legs were spread eagled and a huge blood stain encircled her violated loins. For a long while he lay at her side watching her breasts rise and fall with every breadth, and it was then that he recalled the things Gideon had said. He did not smile as he remembered Gideon's words, and suddenly he realized that Gideon had been wrong in spite of what he had said. He realized this when he saw Maria open her eyes and stare up at the overhead beams, gazing neither right nor left; and she did not spit in his face nor kiss him. Yes, Juan told himself, Gideon had been wrong: instead of accepting or rejecting him she did neither. And this was much worse than *either*! Juan had the strength of five men and the iron will of ten, but when it came to accepting – or facing a future of living with – absolute disregard, of being totally ignored by Maria, this was the one single feeble link in the chain of his personality, the anchor chain to which his masculinity and his potency as a man were linked. There was no way whatsoever for Juan to know during that brief moment of unconscious revelation that it would be only a matter of time before his bride would sever that chain forevermore.

NATCHEZ ON THE MISSISSIPPI
September 3, 1821
Monday
7 a.m.

After mooring the *Panther* south of the city at Greshaw's Landing where Gideon met the vessel after making arrangements for the delivery of the slaves with Rufe Greshaw, dealer in mules and Negroes, who had agreed to act as their agent for an additional five percent over and above the customary auctioneer's fee of ten percent, the gangplank was lowered and Juan went down to the river bank.

'How come Greshaw wants an extra fiver?' Juan demanded, not in an angry tone, but rather, a vexed one.

Gideon's eyes were narrowed as he replied, ' 'Cause we're not white. And also because Greshaw has got to smuggle them in coffles up to the auctioneer's pens so no one will suspect they're Africans fresh off the boat.'

Juan clasped his hands behind his back and stood staring down at the toes of his polished boots. He was dressed in a frock coat and slouch hat of the finest beaver felt, a silk brocaded shirt, and scarlet waistcoat. At his belt, hidden beneath the long coat were his brace of pistols, a dirk, and a fine new Sheffield sword and scabbard. Boko, who was just then descending the gangplank was also dressed in the finest landsmen's mode of the day.

'Did you look in on the missus?' Juan asked as he stopped beside them and turned to look back at the ship to see if the crew was on their toes and watchful, their weapons at the ready.

'Yep,' Boko said. 'She was jest a-sitting and staring off into space, no different from the last time I looked in on her.'

Juan touched Boko's arm when approaching horses were heard racing along the river road. Gideon stepped off the wooden planks of the landing and peered down the road.

After a minute he nodded at Juan and Boko. 'It's all right. That's Greshaw and three wagons a-coming.'

'Only three?'

A man astride a brown chestnut mare cantered into view and doffed his white planter's cap. 'Cap'n Gomez, Ah presume?'

Juan snapped his heels to and bowed stiffly.

The horseman, a tall white man with grey sideburns and a high forehead, stepped from the horse and stood, snapping a riding crop against his boot, peering curiously at the Negro captain and then his vessel beyond them, ten yards from where they stood.

'Ah have three wagons, suh. Ah kin pack fifty niggers into each wagon.'

'I've one hundred seventy-two head aboard,' Juan said. 'Had some bad luck on the middle passage. Ran into a storm and lost five overboard.'

'That's amazing!' Greshaw said, gazing up at the vessel and walking slowly toward it.

'What's that?' Juan asked.

'That you didn't lose more niggers than that. You must run a pow'ful clean and tidy vessel, suh. Sure cain't smell no foul stink like some ships whut lands theah slaves heah.'

Just as the wagons came into the clearing and began to halt at the landing, Juan whistled through his teeth at the men guarding the Negroes whom they had sitting in long queues on deck, hidden from view of the shore because they were made to sit concealed, their backs against the bulwarks. 'Start trotting them down,' Juan said.

The Negroes, anxious to depart from the cramped, overcrowded vessel, stood up and began to shuffle down the plank. Their heads had been shorn and they had been given grey osnaburg shirts and trousers which Boko had purchased as they passed through New Orleans.

At the sight of the robust, healthy and smiling slaves, Greshaw puffed in amazement. 'Suh!' he turned to congratulate Juan, 'them's the best looking prime niggers landed heah as far back as Ah kin recollect. Won't have no trouble fetching maybe eleven, twelve hunnert a head. And wowee, lookit them purty wenches.' The girls and women, bandannas wrapped around their heads and gingham dresses so new the sizing was still stiff as fresh starch, came trotting down the plank. The drivers at the wagons, standing beside the unchained tailgates, bullwhips and blacksnakes coiled in their hands, seemed rather taken aback to see such an orderly, well-disciplined lot of slaves disembark without the need for lashing them.

When all had been loaded into the wagons, twenty young men were lined up in a double file and told to trot alongside them when the wagons started. Juan, Boko, and Gideon boarded the lead wagon and the driver snapped his whip and they were off.

Less than an hour later they arrived at the vendue block where the sale was to be held promptly at nine o'clock that morning. A number of fancily dressed planters and speculators were already on the scene, anxious to have a look at the newly arrived blacks. Juan and Gideon descended from the wagon and stationed themselves in the shadows of a shed far back from the auctioneer's block where they settled down for a long wait.

As they breakfasted on plates of bacon and strong coffee which Greshaw had graciously sent to them on a tray carried by a boy, Boko remained with the coffle as they were being sorted into the stable-like pens behind the vendue block. When all heads had been counted and the tally checked, Boko strolled over to the gathering crowd of bidders and eavesdropped on the sidelines.

Promptly at the appointed hour the auctioneer and his assistants mounted the block and tolled the brass bell. The crowd collected in front of him and the first of some three hundred fifty Negroes being sold that day was trotted around to demonstrate his soundness, and then ordered to stand on the platform and remove shirt and trousers. The bidding was brisk and five minutes later the hammer fell, twelve hundred twenty dollars was the top bid, and the Negro was tagged with the name of his new owner and his lot number and led to the sold pen.

When the first lot was gone, the slaves Juan and his crew had brought were next to go on sale, with the wenches going on the block last in order to hold the continued interest and attention of the big spenders in the audience. No auctioneer worth his salt put his best merchandise on the block first until all the less desirable goods had been disposed of.

It had been prearranged between Gideon, Juan and Boko, that Boko would handle the settling of accounts and then would return to the ship alone, with Gideon and Juan bringing up the rear, following at a distance close enough to defend him against highwaymen or others similarly disposed.

At the conclusion of the sale, which the three men followed with avid interest, and which resulted in a net sale total amount of two hundred sixteen thousand dollars, Boko and the auctioneer's men loaded the money bags in a wagon and hurried away, leaving the Negro and a white driver to make the journey back to Greshaw's landing by themselves.

Juan and Gideon, who had deliberately kept out of sight during the sale and settlement later, at once departed too, following Boko upon horses they had rented at a nearby livery.

When they reached a dense wood about midway between the auctioneer's and the landing shots suddenly rang out from somewhere ahead. Juan and Gideon spurred their animals and raced through the woodland. They came into view of the wagon just as two men were climbing into it.

Drawing his pistols, Juan dashed ahead of Gideon and galloped to within several feet of the wagon, hanging back on the reins and standing in the stirrups to take careful aim. He fired at point-blank range and struck the first highwayman with a clean shot between the eyes. The second man whirled and fired at Juan. The bullet whizzed harmlessly by as Juan aimed his second gun and fired. He missed the man. Then he jerked the reins of the horse, wheeled about, and leaped off the saddle and onto the wagon, hurling himself bodily at the culprit. They tumbled to the ground. Juan, falling on top of the man, took advantage of this and knocked him unconscious with a vicious blow of his knee to the man's groin.

He climbed to his feet and whirled around, looking for Boko. Then he saw him, crumpled in a lifeless heap a few yards off to one side of the road. Juan ran to his side but saw it was too late. Boko had been obviously cut down from ambush. A musket ball had shattered the back of his head. Nearby lay the white man who had driven the wagon. He was dead also.

Standing up with tears unabashedly flowing from his eyes, Juan drew his sword and returned to the unconscious highwayman. He nudged the man with the toe of his boot and turned him over on his back. Gideon, who had dismounted after seeing Boko's corpse, walked over and spat down on the man. 'As I live and breathe!' Gideon hissed. 'It's Hanging Hugh. This murderous jackal was supposed to have died when Gaspar's ship went down.'

'He'll die now, that's for damn sure,' Juan said, kicking the man, then spitting on his face.

Hugh sputtered and groaned and then sat up. He peered at Gideon and recoiled as though he had just been face to face with the devil. 'Gid!' he whispered, 'what're you doing here?'

'You goddamn bilge scum!' Gideon said, kicking him in the teeth. 'You're going to pay for what you did, for shooting Boko in the back like you did – '

Juan's blade rested against Hugh's cheek. The man, wild-eyed with fear, lay back and down on the dirt road. The point of the blade laid open a long shallow cut from corner of his eye to the point of his chin. Gideon's blade flashed in the sunlight and then came to rest on the opposite cheek. He made a deeper cut across Hugh's face than did Juan. The white man groveling on the ground began to sob and incoherently beg for mercy.

'Now you'll die the death of a thousand cuts!' spat Juan, whipping his blade quickly over Hanging Hugh's clothing, cutting away the buttons, slashing through the cloth, opening the seams, and bit by bit, shredding the garments from his body.

Minutes later, the bloodied naked man rolled over and over in the dirt trying to escape. He could not stand and make a run for it because Gideon had cut off his boots and had made numerous criss-crossed cuts on the soles of his feet.

Hugh's blood gushed from the myriad of cuts all over his body, staining the dust, and then turning it into a scarlet pool of mud. The two Negroes stood on either side of the whining, whimpering blackguard at their feet, mercilessly puncturing every inch of his body with the points of their razor-sharp swords. Gideon slashed off his nose, then an ear. Juan whipped his blade lightly down over his belly, laying open the skin from armpit to naval, then with a single swish of his blade, he emasculated him.

Screaming in horror and agony, clutching the bloody stump where his genitals had been, Hugh's heavyset figure jerked and twitched on the ground. Juan cursed and using his blade as a skewer, plucked up the man's dismembered penis on the point and dropped it into his screaming mouth. Then he mashed his boot down upon Hugh's mouth, forcing him to choke almost to death on his own member.

It took a long time for Hanging Hugh to die, and when he finally expired, it was because he had bled to death, not because either Juan or Gideon had mercifully put him out of his misery.

Leaving his mutilated butchered corpse for the vultures and other woodland predators, Juan and Gideon gently lifted Boko's corpse to the wagon and continued on the way back to the ship.

They got under way immediately and headed southward for the mouth of the Mississippi and the Gulf of Mexico beyond.

The next day all hands assembled amidships and stood with bowed heads and tearful eyes as Juan choked over the words of the Lord's Prayer and then ordered Boko's remains committed to the deep. Their voices raised in chorus, singing the hymn Boko had been heard humming to himself so many times down through the years gone by, Gideon and Juan lifted the draped canvas-wrapped body upon the plank and let it slide into the sea.

The day after that they rounded the southern coast of the Florida mainland and put in for Panther Cay. During all this time Juan had not once gone below or entered his cabin in which Maria was locked. He had avoided her like the plague ever since that first night, the night of their wedding, and though he wanted and needed her, he could not bring himself to demand his husbandly privileges again. Because of his grief following Boko's death, Juan was not quite himself and he felt strongly the need for an extended period of idleness ashore.

When the vessel had been moored at the old landing, Juan and Gideon led the men ashore. They walked slowly like men revisiting a burial place. Weeds and underbrush had grown wild over the shelters and the fortification. The cannons had turned to rust from the sea air and the hurricanes which had buried them under salt water and spray and sand and then uncovered them again.

Juan explored the shambles of their crude shelters and when he emerged from his solitary meanderings, he found Gideon and the crew assembled in the clearing, squatting on their heels in the sand.

When Juan approached the men looked up as though unable to decide amongst themselves which one would give him a piece of bad news.

Juan somehow seemed to understand their thoughts. He sensed what they wished to do and he said it for them. 'Men, we've enough to tide us over for quite a spell. Why don't we each go our separate ways and return here, say in six month's time? Make it the first of March.'

Surprised glances were exchanged. Gideon straightened up and squinted at Juan. 'What about you, Panther John?'

Juan shrugged. 'I'll stay here. Perhaps Maria and I can come to an understanding,' he said tiredly. 'Maybe after six months things will change.'

'Maybe,' Gideon said. 'I hope so. I'm kind of looking forward to seeing my woman again. She lives on Matecumbe Key, you know.'

'Yes, I remember.'

'The others want to go their separate ways too. Jacques and Billy have folks in Tampa. Michel and Pierre and the others would like to leave with me in the gig. Will it be all right if we take it and Billy and Jacques borrow the longboat?'

'Yes, of course.'

'That'll leave you with the sailing punt. If you and Maria want to cross the bay to the Florida mainland, it's just right for that.'

'I'm certain we won't wish to do that.'

The others were anxious to get started. They arose and returned to the ship in ones and twos, all of them walking with heavy hearts.

Juan was the last to go aboard. He stood at the rail beside the gangway and shook each man's hand as he emerged later, burdened down with belongings and specie. Juan reminded each man to be certain to have on his person the papers which he had forged for them which certified they were free Negroes and not runaway slaves. During those turbulent days, black men traveling about in the Land of the Free had to carry papers to prove they were not slaves.

Gideon was the last to depart. He tarried for a while to bid Juan farewell. Then the two men embraced and wept unashamedly. Gideon said, as he descended the gangplank, 'I'll be back, old friend, on the first of March. Take care of yourself.'

Juan did not watch them as they left in the two boats which they had lowered over the side from the davits shortly before their departure. He slowly went across the deck and descended the ladder to the companionway leading to his cabin. He removed the key from around his neck and unlocked the door. Maria was sitting on the window seat, staring out at the glassy sea and the mangrove island across the narrow channel.

Juan went over to her and sat down. He took her hand in his and noticed it was cold. Then he lifted her hand to his lips and kissed it gently. There was no response. Maria continued as before, a woman in a catatonic state, immobile, silent, utterly and completely unconscious of everything and everyone about her.

'Come, my dear,' Juan said softly, 'let me show you my island.' He pulled her to her feet and she followed woodenly, staring vacantly ahead. He led her through the door and then helped her up the ladder. On deck in the bright sunshine she blinked and looked around her, somewhat like a person in a state of bewilderment and confusion, but still she did not speak.

Juan led her across the deck and down the gangplank. They walked along the sandy path leading up to the clearing and he showed her around, but if she heard his words or if she saw the things he showed her, she gave no sign, no indication she understood or was aware of who she was, who they were, and where they were.

He led her into the longhouse which had been his quarters during the years he had spent using the island as a hideout. He dusted off the sand and some crisp palm fronds which had turned brown from age from the seat of the chair, the chair he had taken from that sugar plantation in Martinique. Then he led her to the chair and she sat down, stiffly, unmoving, oblivious to him and the room they were in and the rays of the sun streaming through the crumbling spaces in the thatched roof over their heads.

Juan knelt at her side and felt the sand covered carpet under his knees as he rested his head on her lap and then placed her soft white hands upon the top of his head. Suddenly, Juan felt a great sob welling up from deep inside. He knotted his great fists and with his head buried in her lap, felt tears trickling from the corners of his eyes.

It was then, at that moment, that Juan thought he detected for one brief fleeting second, a movement in her hand which was resting upon his neck. He held his breath and waited for her hand to move again, as though perhaps to caress him, but Maria did not move her hand again that day.

PANTHER CAY
October 12, 1821
Sunday
Noon

For thirty-nine days Juan had labored in silence on the island, repairing the buildings, putting the cannon in working order, thatching the roofs, cooking and feeding Maria, reading by night in the great bed he shared with her, swabbing down the *Panther*'s decks every day or so, and in general, keeping so busy physically he was unable to think or occupy his time with forming ambitious plans for the future when Gideon and the men returned.

Day by day he tried to get through to Maria, but nothing he did or said seemed to work. She did not respond to his words, nor his caresses or kisses. She permitted him to feed her, and she allowed him without a word or gesture indicating she knew what he was doing, to bathe her when she soiled herself.

After Juan fed Maria the platter of fried fish and avocado that was their standard fare each noon, he knelt in the sand and stared at her face and body, suddenly losing all patience. He stood up and took her by the hand and pulled her to her feet. Then he walked with her down to the smooth beach. He led her to the water's edge and stopped. This time he was determined not just to bathe her buttocks and genitals, but to strip her naked and take her into the sea with him.

He removed his trousers, tossed his cap aside, and then carefully unbuttoned her dress. When he had removed it, he took off her skirts and then her bodice. She remained standing in the bright sun, naked and still as a white marble statue he had once seen in a Havana museum. As though seeing her as she really was for the first time, Juan began to walk around her, gazing at her blank eyes which as usual continued staring straight ahead, then looking at her rounded breasts, her flowing hips, and her swelling belly.

He stopped dead in his tracks and looked again at her belly. His heart leaped when he realized that moment Maria was growing thick with child – his child. He calculated the time roughly and estimated she was four months; give or take two weeks or so, pregnant.

He told her on bended knee, his hands dark upon her white belly, face uplifted. He told her over and over, 'Maria, heart of my heart, we are to have a child! Our child!'

His words did not reach her. She stood in her trance-like state and did not move.

Juan tenderly embraced her, then led her naked beside him into the sea, his powerfully muscled body, now burned black by the sun, beside her pale soft white body. He held her in his arms and waded out into the warm sea. He floated her upon her back, loving fingers washing her, caressing her. After a few minutes he carried her in his arms to shore and then across the beach to their bed in the longhouse. He placed her gently upon the mattress and laid down beside her, his ear to her belly, listening, straining to hear if there was yet some sign of life.

As Juan lay with ear pressed to her swollen flesh, her hand moved and came to a stop upon his neck. For a long moment he felt the pressure of her hand as though through that gesture, the first she had made during all that time, she was at long last telling him she knew and she understood.

The next day, Maria looked at him once and seemed to smile for a brief moment. The day after that, she did smile. A week later, he felt her fingers in his hand moving, pressing his, as if communicating her feelings.

Christmas Day, Juan brought her some gifts from his sea chest on the ship. There was a new bodice and a bright yellow gown he had never shown her before. As he held the articles up for her to see, she smiled and looked at them and her hand reached forth to touch them, to pinch the cloth of the silk gown between forefinger and thumb. But then she returned to her stoic silence and permitted him to lead her back to bed.

Juan undressed her completely that evening. It was the first time he had seen her totally nude since the day in September when first he discovered her pregnancy.

He slid into bed beside her and rested his head upon her swollen flesh. He felt movement and he heard the heartbeat of the fetus. Joyous, he caressed her, gently, eagerly, his big hands incredibly gentle in their movements. He bent his lips to her breasts and felt the rigidity of her swelling femininity. He lowered his head to her belly again and felt the kickings and movements of the life he had implanted within her. He moved up and kissed her lips, gently, his tongue entering her mouth to embrace her tongue. She responded, ever so slightly, but it was a momentous thrill nevertheless. Throbbing with unrequited desire, Juan kissed her throat, her ears, her breasts, her arm pits, and her belly, gently rolling his tongue around her extended naval, then encircling her loins and thighs and behind her knees, he traveled up again, devouring her with kisses, stroking every inch, every pore of her flesh with his tongue.

Maria sighed and then she did another surprising thing. She raised her hands and placed them on either side of his face. He lifted his gaze and saw tears trickling from her eyes. So overwhelmed was he at that moment, he cried out and encircled her with his arms.

Maria, for the first time in all those months, not only returned his affection, but showed signs of wanting him. He rolled on to his side, taking her with him, cupping her buttocks, encircling his narrow hips with her plump thighs. He felt his throbbing cudgel of flesh threatening to beat against her tender flesh and he clenched his teeth and fought to control the urge. Maria did not utter a sound. She writhed her hips slightly and one tiny hand moved down and touched his member. He felt her fingers grasping him, drawing him to her. He remained frozen, almost paralyzed with apprehension, with the fear that he might hurt her or bring about a miscarriage. But Maria continued to clutch him in her tiny hand. She held him fast and lifted her upper thigh and then eagerly, wantonly, impaled herself upon him.

Juan clenched his hands tighter and tighter upon the voluptuous rounds of her sleek buttocks, but still Maria churned her hips and drove with increasing abandon against him. He held back, he fought with all his will to keep from moving, to keep from letting himself go. Suddenly he felt her go rigid in his arms and her buttocks tightened beneath his fingers, clasping muscles convulsing as she moaned and moaned and moaned, and finally sighed deeply, let her head fall against his chest, and then lay still.

He tried to withdraw from her, but she had her legs locked around his waist. He remained where he was immobile, not daring to move, on the verge of orgasm, and yet, on the brink of some unknown danger.

Hours later Maria lifted her head and gasped. She looked into his eyes for a long while, now seeing him, now telling him something he could not fathom.

'Today is Christmas,' she said, making an observation in a stoic voice, uttering the first words he had heard her speak since that day months before when he had married her.'

'Yes, it is Christmas.'

'And you are my husband.'

'Yes,' he said dryly. 'I am your husband and you are my wife.'

'I am going to have your baby.'

'Our baby. You'll give birth to *our* baby. Our flesh and blood.'

'When?'

'I'm not sure exactly. Toward the end of February, I think.'

'This is December. It was July when you forced me to marry you. The twenty-ninth.'

'I shan't have the baby until April.'

'Are you sure?'

'If this is Christmas Day, then I am sure. I will have the baby on April 6th.'

'You could be wrong.'

'No, I'm right. April 6th. Do you know what to do?'

'Yes. I delivered several suckers.'

'I detest that word. A child is a human being; a person; a baby; a little innocent helpless baby. We shall have a little boy. He will look like you except he will have lighter skin. They will call him a quadroon when he grows up. No?'

'No. A quadroon is the child of a mulatto and a white person. I am not a mulatto. I am a black man.'

'You are a brown man. The sun has burnt you black but your skin will turn pale again if you stay out of the sun.'

'Does the color of my skin offend you?'

'No. But I still insist our child will be lighter than you are and darker than I am. I feel sorry for him if they treat him as a nigger.'

'Perhaps when he grows up the world will be different and color of one's skin won't make a difference.'

'Mixed breeds of any race or animal order are still mongrels,' she said. 'Mongrels are considered lower than bastards, lower than common field niggers, slaves who – '

'I ought to slap you for saying that,' Juan muttered.

She turned her face toward him, eyes blazing with blue flecks of passion, of defiance. 'Go ahead, hit me. Punch me in the belly, kill our little mongrel.'

'If you say that again, if you so much as utter a word like that again,' he said through clenched teeth, shaking his fist in her face, 'I swear I'll – '

'You'll do what, hurt me?'

Juan brought his emotions under control. 'No, I won't hurt you. I'd sooner chop off my hands than bring harm to you.'

She smiled but her eyes were fixed in a strange stare. 'You are my husband and you really do love me very much, don't you?'

'Yes, yes, I do.'

'You love me not nearly as much as I feel for you.'

He frowned. He leaned on an elbow and peered into her blue eyes. 'What do you *feel* for me?'

She did not avert her gaze as she replied, unhesitatingly, unequivocably, 'I feel for you hatred, contempt, loathing. You murdered my father in cold blood. You kidnaped me. You killed innocent men. You raped me. You impregnated me with your black nigger's sperm. I am a white woman; a woman of noble birth who has been enslaved by a blackamoor and kept a prisoner. I hate you, nigger. I pray for the day when I shall pee on your rotting corpse.'

Juan did not feel rage or pain at her words. Instead, he experienced a quality of understanding, not of anger, or indignation, but of faith in the belief that she was speaking in anger and not from the heart. Had she not responded to him only a few hours before? Had she not shown she desired him, that she sought to return the love and the caresses he had given so freely? He decided not to heed her words. He gazed raptly at her and smiled. Then he slid off the bed and got down the small leather bound Bible from a shelf above the window. He carried the Bible reverently to her and placed it upon her belly. Then he took her hand in his and rested it upon the Bible.

She blinked and looked up at him in wonder.

'Swear by this holy book on your – *our* – unborn baby's

life that you acknowledge that I am your husband and you are my wife. Swear it!'

Maria was not frightened nor coerced nor terrorized by the wild look on his face. She looked up at him, disdain contorting the soft contours of her mouth. 'Go to hell.'

'Swear it!' His hand tightened upon hers, crushing her fingers, grinding them into the binding of the holy book.'

She squirmed and then winced. Then, crying out in pain, 'Stop, you're breaking my hand.'

He relaxed his grip but did not release her hand. He stood hovering above her, his hard muscular body gleaming with sweat in the heat of the longhouse like a black marble statue of Apollo.

Maria sighed and her gaze wandered over his nakedness. After a long pause she finally sighed in resignation and nodded, admitting, 'Yes, what's the use? You can't escape reality. I'm your wife and just as certainly as you are the father of my unborn child, I acknowledge you as my husband. I pray God to have pity on me.'

'Swear on this Bible, swear it!'

'All right, you stubborn lout, I swear it! On this Bible I swear it. Now go away and let me alone. When the baby comes and I am on my feet I want you to promise you'll leave this island and never come back again. If you will promise me that, I'll – '

'You'll what?' he asked, tensely, with strong feeling of apprehension. He somehow knew that the conditions with which he had to comply were unfair as much to herself and the unborn baby as they were unfair to himself as well.

'I'll have the child.'

'You mean, you would deliberately harm that infant – ?'

'Haw!' she cried, 'listen to the big bold bad Panther John the pirate! Suddenly he's a saint.'

Juan was unable to stand anymore of her vituperation. He withdrew, leaving the Bible resting on her naked heaving belly. He walked outside into the fading sunlight, naked, feeling the breezes cooling his flesh, wishing that she would have remained as she had been during those past months, mute, immobile, unseeing, instead of recovering. Which had it been that caused her to recover: the need for his love or the need to loathe and despise him?

Juan realized he would never learn the answer. He walked away from the compound and went down to the ship. For a long while he gazed up at it and once again wished he was walking her decks while she soared across the sea, running before the wind, proving herself again and again she could overtake, and then sink, any and all craft afloat.

Juan breathed deeply the free air and he longed to be off the island and far, far away. Then he broke into a hard run, ran up her sloping gangplank after jumping across from the bank, and went down into his cabin. He opened a fresh keg of rum and then eased himself into his bunk with the open tap just above his mouth.

As he lost himself to the world of reality, Juan knew he was destined to some unknown fate: a fate that not even Boko, were he still alive, could foretell. He tried to imagine the son Maria would have. He wanted to see him in his own image; he wished for nothing else, except his son. 'Juan Gomez, my son, the son of Panther John!' he shouted at the top of his voice.

Staggering to his feet, sending the keg bouncing and rolling across the deck, sending its dark contents spurting in rivulets into crevasses and cracks between the deck planks, Juan went to his desk and began to rummage about for quill and ink. When he found them, he sat upon the edge of the chair, ripped a sheet of parchment from one of his log books, and carefully, painstakingly, began to write, *'On this Christmas Day, 1821, I, Captain Juan Gomez, also known as Panther John, the pirate, do hereby bequeath, to my son who has as yet to be born and who is expected to be born on the 6th day of April in the year of our Lord, 1822, all my earthly goods and worldly possessions, which may be found buried on Panther Cay, at "X" on the map hand drawn below; and also on the other cays and islands this map doth show.'*

Juan surveyed his handiwork and then began the laborious task of accurately portraying the islands in map form. When he was finished, he got down his jewel box and took from it a tiny amulet upon a neck chain. The amulet was made of gold in the figure of a saint with one hand held aloft as though in blessing the congregation of a church. Juan then unscrewed the arm from the miniature statue, rolled the parchment into a tiny scroll, and slipped it into the cavity. He replaced the arm and after screwing it down tightly, lit an alcohol lamp and heated the metal so the statue-amulet appeared to be made of one piece of solid gold.

Then Juan blew out the lamp, hung the amulet around his

neck, and collapsed upon the bunk, vowing that on the morrow he would rebury his treasure at the places he had marked on the map for his unborn son to someday find.

PANTHER CAY
March 1, 1822
Thursday
Early Afternoon

Juan was aloft atop the mainmast, glass to his eyes, scanning the horizon in every direction. During the months that passed following Maria's recovery, the two of them completely avoided each other's company. To keep his mind occupied, Juan busied himself with carpenter's tools aboard the *Panther*. When every peg had been tested and loose plank healed and caulked, and when every fitting had been greased, every rotted line replaced, every sail repaired and aired and checked, and fresh pitch applied to her hull where needed, Juan went aloft with glass in hand, to await the return of his crew.

Each day, just as he so diligently scanned the horizon in expectation of his men, he also observed, from afar, the progress of his wife's swelling belly. Time hung heavy on his shoulders. He was fresh again and aching for action. He wanted to vent his strangling passions with cutlass in hand. But he knew he could not until after he had delivered Maria of his son; and until he had arranged for her to have a servant to care for him and protect him during his absences.

Sitting astride the rope-bound platform of the crow's nest that afternoon, Juan rested his head against the mast and closed his eyes, feeling the wind in his beard, tasting the salt tang of the sea upon his lips. Though he had more specie than he could ever hope to spend, somehow it meant nothing to have so many thousands of dollars in treasure. All he craved was the adventure, the challenge, the hunt, of searching for more. His acquisitiveness was not motivated by greed or need; instead it was impelled by the need to acquire, to seek and destroy those who held the wealth collected from the indigent and poor of the world, for that was where and from whom great fortunes and small were always obtained:

from the powerless, the ignorant, the poor man. As to how Juan came to this conviction cannot be said, except that it was the sort of thing a man who has been enslaved seems to know and understand through instinct alone.

Juan rested his head and absently watched Maria as she wallowed behind her bulging stomach down to the spring at which she had spread her garments to dry after scrubbing them early that day in the coolness of morning. He could not fathom this vile-tongued white woman, nor could he undertake any longer to win or earn her affection. The challenge of the quest existed no more. Only the challenge of the quest at sea was real to Juan; only *that* was now all that mattered.

Suddenly, from somewhere in the east he glimpsed a momentary brightness, like a mirror flashing in the sun. He felt his heart leap as he climbed to his feet and bracing the open spyglass against the mainmast, slowly focused the lens on the far horizon.

Then he saw it, the sail of a small boat. He squinted through the eyepiece and watched as the boat on the horizon drew nearer. He made out her lines. She was the gig. A quarter hour later he could count the figures in the boat. At the helm sat Gideon. Beside him on either side of the craft sitting along the hull were eight men – his returning crew!

Juan opened the semaphore stowage box and removed the handmirror. He lifted it and flashed the recognition signal. Then he returned the glass to his eye and watched as Gideon, sitting aft with the tiller under his elbow, returned the signal.

At this, Juan snapped the rings of the glass, telescoping it and shoved it in his pocket. Then he grabbed a hold on the main chains and slid all the way down to the deck in one swift spiraling descent. He went below and returned carrying ten tin cups and a firkin of dark rum. He spread an awning above the deck just forward of the mainmast and set out the cups and the unopened firkin. Then he ran forward and walked out on the end of the bowsprit to await their arrival.

That evening Gideon and the eight men who returned with him sat around the oil lantern drinking and catching up on events. Most of them had returned broke, all except Michel and Pierre, who had buried most of their specie on the island before they departed. Gideon had left a large share of his money with a former wife and then he took the rest of it and spent it in Savannah on five months of riotous living during which time he lived with three wenches at the same time. The others recanted similar adventures, and when they talked themselves out, it was Gideon who brought up the question, 'Capitaine Juan, what next?'

Juan emptied his cup in a single gulp and leaned back against the bulkhead, arms folded behind his head. 'I've done a lot of thinking these past months. Now that Maria is about due, I think we ought to fetch her a woman servant so she can be left here with the child; then we can go anywhere we like, and do anything that suits us.'

The men grinned round at each other. It was the old Panther John talking, saying the words they had been longing to hear.

Michel grinned and suggested, 'The waters around New Providence are teeming with rich merchantmen.'

'Naw,' cried Bernay, a slight mulatto who had once served as messboy aboard a British frigate with the Royal Navy. 'Them warters are a mite unhealthy. Too many cruisers American and British to suit the likes o'me.'

'The danged best of all is slave tradin',' said George, a black ex-slave who had successfully escaped a plantation before he found his way to Havana and then to the Isle of Pines where he joined Panther John's crew.

Everyone nodded in agreement. Juan smiled and said, 'Let's vote on it, gentl'men. All those in favor of slaving – ?'

All hands said aye.

'All those in favor of making another trip to Africa – ?'

The men remained silent.

Juan looked at them, questioning their decision with a puzzled frown.

Gideon dipped his cup into the half empty firkin and swished it around before putting the rim to his lips. He sipped several swallows, smacked his lips, then told Juan, 'We talked it over and decided the voyage is too risky and wearisome, what with the long time it takes and the danger of running into storms or war ships. Therefore, we have a better idear. Why not let others buy the slaves for us? Then all we have to do is overtake them, kill the crews, and sell the slaves ourselfs.'

Juan smiled with hearty approval. He scratched his beard and then said, 'Very well, then that is what we shall do!'

After they drank to that, Juan said, 'Since we can't cast off until next month anyhow because I want to be here when the baby comes, and since we ought to go about this by using spies to tip us off about the comings and goings of the slavers, I think we each ought to take off in different directions. One of us to St Augustine, another to Charleston, a third to Savannah, a fourth man to Natchez, a fifth to New Orleans, and a sixth to Havana.'

Gideon was immensely pleased. 'An excellent plan, cap'n. Then it's agreed – ?' he paused looking around at each face. The men were nodding in vigorous acceptance. Gideon smiled and said, 'Good. We leave in the morning on the gig. We shall return in a month not only with a network of spies ashore who will agree to tell us what we want to know, but with some able bodied fighting men to put some more muscle in our crew.'

Juan smiled. He toasted the others and Gideon, drank his fill, then went below, beckoning for Gideon to accompany him. When they were in Juan's cabin, he produced a pouch from a hiding place above a beam and placed it in Gideon's hand. 'This is for expenses – and money to buy a healthy woman, white preferably, to serve Maria and the child.'

PANTHER CAY
April 2, 1822
Monday
Early Morning

The woman Gideon bought in the slave market at Charleston was a flaxen haired buxom talkative soul of eighteen who was utterly delighted to have a new mistress who lived all alone on an island. However, when she saw the crude buildings, and the primitive way of life she threw herself upon the beach in a fit of hysteria, kicking her chubby legs into the air and pounding the sand with her fists.

The screaming fit ended a short while afterward as soon as Maria went into labor. Then Hilda, the flaxen haired slave, came to her senses and went right to work. By eight o'clock that same evening, a chubby, fair skinned baby boy emerged in the world of Panther Cay and a celebration was held shortly thereafter. Three days following the birth of Juan junior, the father placed the golden amulet around the child's neck, bid him adieu, and sailed off with his crew in haste because they had a rendezvous to intercept a slave ship which was at that moment en route to New Orleans.

Bright and early on the morning of the seventh, Saturday, Juan's crew, which now consisted of seven new recruits who had joined them after having sailed with several of Lafitte's former captains, caught sight of the slaver and at once proceeded to overtake her.

The slave ship, a sloop of French design tried her best to outrun the swift *Panther*, but within two hours the stench of the chained cargo below decks was pungent in the nostrils of Juan and his crew. Juan cursed the stubborn master of the slaver for continuing the flight even though it was by that time obvious they would be overtaken within another hour. He climbed aloft with trumpet in hand and shouted vainly for the slaver to heave to. The slaver ignored him.

At this slight, Juan shouted for the gun crew to man their

stations. He swung down from the rigging upon a free line and landed lightly on his feet at the helm. He dismissed the helmsman and took the wheel himself. Then he brought the bow around and shouted for the starboard crew to take aim. A moment later, Juan shouted, 'Fire!'

The guns thundered in unison, belching flame, smoke, and iron dumbbell shot into her rigging. The shot ripped gaping rents in her canvas and felled the shrouds and tops'ls. Crippled, but still trying to evade the pirates, the captain ordered his men to break out their weapons and commence firing. Juan, burning with rage, shouted from the rigging, 'Kill every white sonofabitch aboard. Stand by with boarding pikes, *board*!'

At that, the crew swarmed over the side, screaming in rage as they fell upon the motley crew who manned the slaver. Short work was made of them. Juan, burning with rage because the slaver master had not surrendered, caught the man trying to go over the side and get into a dingy he had cut loose, and brought him amidships. The two vessels were made fast together, then the Negro slaves below decks were brought up. The slaves, manacled and chained together by a continuous length of leg irons, were sent aboard the *Panther*, one by one, their bodies weakened by dysentery and scurvy, their flesh infected with sores and yaws. It was necessary for the crew of the *Panther* to help them across for they were so weak and ill few had strength enough for such exertion.

Juan counted the slaves. There were eighty-four He slapped the captain's red face several times and demanded to know how many slaves he had loaded aboard and where.

'Two hundred ninety, suh,' came the reply. 'We bought'n them from a Portugee trader bunch at Bissagos Island off'n the coast of Africy near the Sierra Leone country.'

'And this is all what's left? Gideon asked, incredulous.

The man grunted and nodded.

Gideon and Juan exchanged fiery glances. Juan spat into the captain's face and shouted to his crew, 'Truss this bastard for keel hauling.'

As soon as the slaves had been secured aboard the *Panther*, the slaver captain was placed in irons and then the irons were fixed to a long cable which was thrown over the side and under the keel where it was brought up the other side, then attached to the bottom of his cage-like trusses.

All hands came on deck and began wagering how many

times Juan would order him under the keel, across the barnacle-encrusted hull, and then up to the deck again. Bets were placed that the captain would not survive the first go round.

The man was hurled screaming into the sea. The crew ran to the side and watched as he slid under the waves going around the hull. The crew manning the cables, heaved, pulled, and pulled until the sopping captain appeared, feet first, out of the water alongside the hull on the starboard side.

Those who wagered he would not survive the first keel hauling, paid off their bets. The man was dragged across the deck, regurgitating sea water, algae, and the meal he had eaten for breakfast all over the decks, much to the derision of the men.

He was dropped over the starboard side a second time, but on this go round, the cables became snarled and his manacled body caught somewhere on the keel. Ten minutes elapsed before the crews heaving on the cables managed to work him loose and haul his remains up the port side. They pulled until he emerged feet first, but when the men saw what the sharks had done to him, Michel ran forward with a cutlass and cut loose the cables.

As they released the slave ship from the long line to which they had her tied in tow, Juan loaded the eighteen pounder with cannister he had first dipped in whale oil, and then got off the first shot. The cannister burst open upon the deck of the ill-fated slaver and set her ablaze. The crew shouted with glee as Juan continued his handiwork, now with round shot which he aimed and fired, volley after volley, at the water line of the burning ship.

Finally, in a great wallowing belch of flame and hissing smoke, the slaver's bow slid heavenward, she seemed to shudder for a moment as though afraid of her fate in the watery grave below, and then slipped beneath the waves amid a great hissing forth of smoke and steam and churning, bubbling sea.

Juan, Gideon, and Pierre, who had some medical training when he served with Napoleon, looked over the motley lot of sick and dying slaves and decided it would be unwise to offer them for sale in such poor condition.

It was agreed that the slaves would be brought to Panther Cay where they would be fed, housed, clothed, and treated before being taken to the slave mart. Once this was decided, Juan put about and the vessel headed home.

When they were within sixty-five miles of the Florida coast, an American man o'war under full sail appeared on the horizon from the west. The vessel was sailing like a gigantic winged porpoise leaping over the waves right after them, hot on their trail.

Juan swung aloft and peered at the warship through his glass. What he saw was enough to turn his stomach over. The vessel, a swift three decker with at least forty guns which before long would be within range of their deck, was rapidly overtaking the *Panther*. Juan shouted commands to trim the sails, but it was soon evident such efforts were to no avail. The warship's huge guns would blast them out of the water. They had but one hope, to lighten her load in order to trim the craft so she would make better time under her canvas. Juan stood peering at the warship, his glass resting upon the mizzen stays. Gideon came up behind him and pressed his shoulder. 'What do you think, cap'n?'

'Bring the niggers topside and secure that long chain that their leg irons are hooked to, secure it – '

'To what, cap'n?'

Juan looked at Gideon. Though it was cool and a moderate breeze was stirring up whitecaps, sweat was dripping from Juan's face. ' – to the anchor.'

Gideon understood the command. If they could lighten the ship they had a fair chance of outdistancing the larger, heavier vessel whose taller masts, larger sails, and enormous top royals reached the stronger thermals then churning invisibly across the sea. Moreover, in the event they were overtaken, there would be no evidence aboard that the *Panther* was being used for smuggling slaves.

Suddenly, Juan understood the reason why the slave ship captain had affixed each slaves leg iron at three-foot intervals to one long single heavy iron chain. No doubt he too had considered the possibility of jettisoning an entire cargo of slaves in the event he was overtaken and facing capture.

Juan did not look round as the chains of the seemingly endless coffle of Negroes was heard clanking and dragging across the deck. Juan continued to stare at the warship through his glass, occasionally pausing to calculate the distance between the two vessels with the quadrant – the quadrant Maria Dunsmore's captain had used that day when the

Panther had overtaken them. Suddenly, Juan began to laugh. He thought about all the fish in the sea. The little ones got eaten up by bigger fish, and the bigger fish were devoured by still bigger fish; and finally, bigger ones ate them. It was an endless cycle of life and death. Now he felt like the shark being pursued by the whale; the killer whale; but was not Jonah rescued from the belly of the whale?

Juan turned and watched the forward crew as they finished securing the coffle of slaves to the heavy starboard anchor. He barked a command to the helmsman to bring the bow fifteen degrees to the east in order to conceal what they were about to do from the watchful spyglasses of the officers aboard the pursuing warship. This done, Juan shouted, 'Lash them niggers against the bulwarks. Swiftly there, now line 'em up. Already to cut loose the anchor. Cut!'

Gideon and a crewman fell upon the heavy cable with their cutlasses, hacking the blades down as rapidly as they could strike. In a trice there was a scraping rumble and the anchor, freed of its cables, rode down the lurching timbers of the hull and with a gigantic splash plummeted into the sea, dragging with it, the screaming chain of frantically struggling slaves. All eighty-four Negroes disappeared beneath the sea in less than thirty seconds and though they had vanished so swiftly, their blood-curdling screams continued to echo on the wind and in the crew's ears long afterward. Juan, spitting up bile, looked aft again and took another reading with the quadrant.

To his relief he saw that the *Panther* was beginning to pull away from the warship. Then he ordered a jug of rum be brought to the quarterdeck, and settled himself comfortably like an acrobat upon the taffrail, legs crossed, the rolling sea at times splattering him from below, as he sat swigging from the jug and shaking his fist at the slowly shrinking sails astern.

ISLE OF PINES, CUBA
May 1, 1833
Thursday
2 p.m.

Gideon frowned and halted Juan before they entered the island grog shop. He nodded in slow deliberation, protesting what they were about to do. 'Mark my words, *mon ami*, before this day is over we will cross swords with Calico Jack and his crew of cut-throats.'

Juan rested a hand on the hilt of the cutlass swinging from his belt. He contemplated Gideon's dark face and black expression with amusement. 'Since when does my first officer run from a good fight?'

'I am not running. Any fight with Calico Jack and his lot does not promise to be a good one. If anything, it will be bad for us – if we do not watch our steps.'

'Gideon, you are getting old,' observed Juan.

'If it is wrong to exercise caution, sar,' Gideon said with a touch of irony, 'then I apologize for being cautious.'

'I won't argue the point,' Juan said. 'But why this concern about Calico Jack now? In all the years we've been coming here to sell our cargoes, never once have we had trouble with him or his crew.'

Gideon's eyes were intent in an annoyed stare of anger and chagrin. 'Have you forgotten, sar, that was in the old days when we lived by the code of the brotherhood – when Lafitte was keeping the peace here. But now that the brotherhood is no more, and now that honorable pirates no longer sail to this free port, we would be fools *not* to expect trouble.'

'All right,' Juan said. 'We'll settle our business with Quesado as soon as the men are finished loading the goods aboard his packet and then we'll be off.' He turned to enter the noisy and smoke-filled grog shop but again Gideon caught his arm and stopped him.

Annoyed, Juan turned and glared.

Before Juan could say anything, Gideon shook his head and said, 'Heed me, Juan. Don't go in there. That's asking for trouble. Calico Jack and his whole motley crew are inside – waiting for *you.*'

Gideon's warning to John was not without reason. Juan recalled the old days, when they all had been sailing under Gaspar's flag. He recalled how the tall mulatto buccaneer had always swaggered on the decks in such a way that Juan was forced to step aside in order to avoid him. Once, when Juan was bringing a hot toddy on a silver tray up to Leon Gaspar who was on the quarterdeck of the *Mer Jewel* at the time, Calico Jack deliberately tripped him. The moment Juan made a gesture as though to hurl himself in rage at the mulatto buccaneer, Calico drew his cutlass and started slashing at the unarmed slave. At the memory of what had happened that day so many years before, Juan stood staring into space, recalling with clarity as though it had only happened that day and not so long ago the emotions he had felt surging through him. It was Gideon who had saved his life when he jumped from the taffrail and pinned Calico Jack's arms to his sides until Gaspar could intercede and order him to cease and desist. Juan recalled Leon Gaspar's words: 'Put up your blade, Jack. He's the best body servant I ever had, even if he is a black bastard. Don't run him through – his blood is so onerous it'll rust your blade.'

Calico Jack had stood there, glaring at Juan and at Gideon, the slave who had had the audacity to lay his hands on him. He spat into Juan's face and laughed, saying, 'The hour will come, niggers, when you'll have to answer for what you just did. Calico never forgets.'

Juan recalled with regret and bitterness the many occasions since that day when he had found himself face-to-face with Calico Jack, and he remembered that each time he had made a move to cross blades with the swaggering mulatto, Gideon had always been there to stop him. Then, as now, Gideon was Juan's guardian and mentor, though it was a self-appointed role; and then, as now, he once again was attempting to discourage him and stop him from the inevitable clash in a duel with Calico Jack which every freebooter of the day knew was as certain to be and as inevitable as the rising and falling of the tides.

Juan also realized Gideon was right; that Calico Jack and his crew were probably at that very moment plotting to settle the score with them as well as planning to attack his crew and capture the *Panther*. He *knew* Gideon was right because they had spied several of Calico Jack's crew watching as they began the tedious job of unloading the cargo from the holds and decks of the *Panther* and then loading it aboard Quesado's vessel, the Cuban-built sailing packet: Moreover, Juan realized that things had changed since the pirate brotherhood had disbanded and the last vestiges of civilized order had vanished from the Isle of Pines. Only the bloodthirstiest of the pirates who sailed the waters of the Caribbean and the Gulf of Mexico remained – and visited the now lawless port town of Neuva Gerona where they had landed only a few hours before. Despite this, Juan was determined to settle the old score. During the years, he had not forgotten the humiliation he had suffered that day when Calico Jack had deliberately provoked him into going against him – and he had not forgotten the terrible blow to his pride when Gideon had risen to help him – at peril of his own life. It was the one singular event in his life as a slave that Juan remembered with remorse – and vowed that one day when the opportunity arose, he would make the most of that opportunity to avenge his pride and personal honor. Now that the time had come, Juan was not to be deterred. Gideon could no longer hold him back – even if it meant going up against Calico Jack and his entire crew as well – singlehandedly – he would see the thing through.

From the expression on Juan's face, Gideon understood the thoughts in the young man's mind: he knew he had to stand up to Calico Jack even if the odds were stacked against him. That was the way Juan was – that was why he had earned the name *Panther John*. He was as fierce and relentless as the panther who attacks an enemy. 'All right,' Gideon said with a troubled shrug. 'I'll go in with you. But first let me signal the crew. I think we could use a few trusty hands to back us up.'

Juan grinned. He loosened the cutlass at his side in the hanger and said, 'Old friend, remember one thing. Calico Jack is *mine*. No matter what happens, don't interfere. He will taste *my* steel and no one else's. Do I make myself understood?'

Gideon nodded. He turned and trotted down to the quay. He looked up at the gangway and caught the sideboy's eye. The man swung down on a tackle line, listened briefly and stoic-faced to what Gideon had to say, then returned to the deck to carry out the orders he had just received. Several minutes later the crew began to file off the vessel singly, and in pairs, weapons concealed, their manner easy and nonchalant as though nothing was the matter.

Juan waited until he had seen the sideboy return to the ship to spread the word amongst the crew. Then he turned and entered the grog shop, walking, as though without a care in the world, toward the tables in the main saloon where Calico Jack, his crew, and the crews of several other pirate ships in the harbor, were carousing. The din, the smoke of hashish and tobacco, of cooking grease and grog, the stench of unwashed bodies and foul breaths, all this surrounded Panther John like some unreal blanket of smell and sound and sensation of which he was only vaguely aware. Through the haze and the blur of faces he saw the leering, broad-nostriled face of Calico Jack beaming at him in hatred like a pale tan mask. For the life of him, Juan had never understood why Jack had taken such an intense dislike to him. But whatever the reason, this was no time for thinking of that now.

Around him, Juan was aware of the seamen at the tables turning to stare. As he calmly, purposefully, seated himself at a table and found himself face-to-face with Calico Jack who was seated at the adjacent table, the laughter and shouting in the room ceased, as all hands strained to watch and listen. Rapidly, a silence pervaded the entire grog shop.

The tension was electric in the air. For months the crew of Calico Jack's ship had been conjecturing and whispering amongst themselves about the inevitable showdown between their captain and Panther John. They came to know this when Calico Jack one night came storming on deck, a bottle of rum in one fist and his cutlass in the other, swearing he would have Panther John's head.

When asked why he had suddenly announced this intention, Calico Jack smashed the rum bottle upon the deck and shouted: 'Because that nigger bastard is ruining these waters for us legitimate pirates, that's why. Of late the pickings have been so poorly we 'uns is left with nothing while he picks off the fattest of prizes. I hear tell he even uses voodoo magic to discover and spy out the routes the fat merchantmen sail. By gar! We can't have this sort of thing, now can we?'

What provoked Calico Jack into making this explosive

outburst was the fact that he had learned, much to his consternation and outrage, that Gaspar's runaway slave had captured six rich prizes during the past few months and was at that very moment, unloading the proceeds of those piratanical forays right under his nose and before the envious eyes of his crew on the quay at Neuva Gerona. Such an affront was tantamount to rubbing Calico Jack's face in it. It was too much for Calico Jack to accept for he had suffered in silence too many years his envy of Panther John. He promptly opened his sea chest, strapped on his cutlass, wrapped his kinky hair in the familiar red and white calico headscarf he always wore as a good luck fetish when duelling or boarding a prize on the high seas, and announced his intention to everyone within earshot and even some who were within hailing distance that he was seeking out Panther John for satisfaction. Although Gideon and others in Juan's crew had been forewarned by pirates of other crews then in the town and on the waterfront, no one had dared step forward to inform Panther John that Calico Jack was about to challenge him. Panther John needed no such warning. He had long expected – and looked forward to this chance to cross blades with his hated rival.

A buxom serving girl with yellow hair and bright blue eyes came from behind the counter carrying tray and wiping cloth. She appraised Juan with a smiling glance and leaned forward to mop the table and remove several empty tankards and the gnawed bones of a lamb's quarter which the prior patrons had left at the table. As she leaned across the table, rapidly scrubbing away the crumbs and grease and spilled ale, she said in a cautious whisper, 'The proprietor said to warn you – don't look now, sir – but there is a plot afoot to do you in.'

Juan grinned. His gaze for a moment moved from her face and rested upon her full ripe breasts peeking tiredly from beneath the front of her bodice as she scrubbed the table. Then he reached into his waistcoat pocket and withdrew several gold pieces. He slipped them into her hand, winked, and pinched her rounded buttocks. 'Thank you, my lady. Now fetch me a grog and carry on. I am well aware of what is – '

'Take your black hand off that woman's ass!' came a gravel-voiced shout, interrupting Juan.

It was Calico Jack. He had banged his tankard down upon

the table before him with such force the liquid sloshed all over the planks and the pewter tankard vent and went flying when the handle broke off.

The girl moved hastily aside. Juan sat in his chair, one hand resting on the hilt of his cutlass at his side, the other upon the table top. He confronted Calico Jack from his seat and grinned. 'A plague on you and your scurvy ancestors,' Juan hissed, recalling as he spoke an oriental pirate he had once met there on the Isles of Pines who had constantly uttered that very same curse. He had chosen the words deliberately, for he also recalled, with some measure of satisfaction, that Calico Jack had lost that duel that day when he drew his blade and attacked the oriental pirate. But before the man from the orient could get set to run Calico Jack through with his scimitar after he had pinned his adversary to the bulkhead and had disarmed him, one of Calico Jack's brigands stabbed him in the back. Juan recalled this and smiled, promising himself to be cautious and not for a moment turn his back.

Not bandying words, Calico Jack arose slowly, kicking aside his chair and drawing his blade in one swift motion. In blind rage he brought the cutlass down upon the table. It struck with such force the planks were halved and the table fell away, split neatly down the center.

Juan nimbly moved to his feet, drawing his weapon with such speed it appeared as if by magic in his right fist. The men in the grog shop began to scramble out of the way, dragging chairs and tables and carrying their bottles and tankards to the sides of the room. Several men hastily began to make wagers on which of the two, the mulatto or the black man, would emerge the victor.

From all sides of the room, Juan's crew after entering without being noticed, began to converge, their eyes watching Calico Jack's crew for some sign of interference, their twitching fingers eager upon pistol butt and knife handle.

Jack spat out a string of vile curses in French and Creole as he slashed and lunged toward Juan.

With a laugh, Juan stepped aside and parried Calico Jack's blade with a broadside strike against the steel that landed with such force the room reverberated with the ring of their blades and sparks flew.

Again Calico Jack swung wildly at Juan. And gracefully as before, Juan sidestepped and danced lightly out of range, his weapon held high, his intent eyes fixed upon Jack's light-complexioned broad face. With a cry of rage and a bellow that was intended to startle, Jack again went slashing toward Juan. Juan parried and then with a lightning swift movement, nicked the bigger pirate captain on the arm, drawing the first blood. A hush went over the mob watching and the wagering began anew, in frantic whispers as gold and silver specie of all nationalities changed hands.

During the ensuing several minutes the two men circled, their blades constantly in motion, their footwork nimble. Then Jack cried out at the top of his lungs, a fierce shout that again was calculated to frighten and startle his younger adversary.

In reply, Juan laughed. 'What's the matter, yellar nigger, are you hollering because you're afraid?'

Provoked, almost blind with rage, Calico Jack began slashing and making an advance with unbelievable ferocity. Juan laughed and sidestepped easily, moving backward with the grace of a panther, then finding an opening, stepping in and lightly slashing Calico Jack on the forehead. Boos began to fill the room as Jack's own crew began to jeer at him. They were vexed because they had wagered on their captain and now he was showing signs of losing the duel. The blood flowing from the cut on his forehead poured over his face and partially blinded him in one eye. The first wound, on his arm, was bleeding profusely and blood was dripping all over the puncheon floors and running down his blade.

Juan, continuing to laugh, continuing to think of all the years he had awaited this moment of revenge, and remembering the day many years before when Calico Jack had deliberately provoked him, held himself in check. He wanted to savor every minute of the battle; he wanted to enjoy the thrill of cutting Calico Jack to ribbons before the eyes of his men. Now that he heard for the first time their jeers, he began to take especial delight in proving he was better than the mulatto; the light-skinned pirate of color who had so often and for so long believed himself to be superior to others of his race. Juan stepped nimbly up to a chair and then skipped across several tables, leaping into the air several times a split second before Calico Jack's slashing blade whistled toward his legs.

He jumped down to the floor when Calico was backed into a corner and began to drive at him relentlessly, hoping to wear him down. But Calico Jack was not a weak man and would not be exhausted so soon. He had spent all his life before the mast and behind a blade and too, he had killed more than his share of men who dared cross swords with him. All this, Juan knew. But he also knew that he was the better man and this duel was about to prove it, provided all continued to go well. He did not throw caution to the winds. He knew only too well what one small slip, one small miscalculation in judgment, would make. And he knew that he would of necessity be forced to be wary of every man in the room who was not among those loyal to him and Gideon. Out of the corner of his eye Juan glimpsed Gideon, hovering near the door, both hands resting on the grips of his pistols, the pistols which Juan knew were primed and loaded and cocked. As Juan leapt upon a table again and danced lightly out of range of Calico Jack's slashing blade, he caught a glimpse of several of his men, muskets at the ready, standing at strategic places in the great room. He smiled and continued his evasive action for the moment, toying with the lumbering mulatto who was beginning, at long last, to show signs of wearying as great beads of perspiration began to form on his light-skinned face and mingle with the streaming blood staining the calico headscarf. The bravado and look of smug disdain had long since vanished from Jack's face as everything attempted failed in his furious effort to bring Juan to bay.

He tried several ruses, seizing a chair and hurling it at Juan in an attempt to trip him and get him at a momentary disadvantage, but each time he failed in the effort and received mumblings of disdain from his crew watching. So far as the pirate crew was concerned, a duel between two rival captains was an affair of honor not to be conducted like other combats; but instead to be fought with courage and decorum befitting officers and gentlemen. To see their captain so savage in his anger that he was ignoring the rules of gentlemanly honor by throwing chairs at his adversary was in and of itself a thing of disdain which every man watching believed contemptible. Only Juan remained the officer and gentleman. And only he received the plaudits and low-key compliments as he parried and thrust and fought with courage and expertise. This too was a thing of vexation to Calico Jack. He bellowed in rage when he saw his own men applauding an acrobatic feat of surprising swiftness and agility on Panther John's part; and he also cursed aloud when he realized that some among his crew, mainly those whom he considered beneath himself – those men with the black and brown complexions of the Negro who were not as good as he was – were cheering his adversary on to victory. This was tantamount to open betrayal and Calico Jack shouted at the top of his lungs in rage and frustration, promising he would personally maim and cripple any man in his crew who failed to show their allegiance to himself. This, the men did not like. Glances were exchanged and it became immediately evident that they were weary of Calico Jack's mistreatment and were avidly wishing that Panther John would soon do him in.

Backing against a corner and quickly shoving a keg of rum toward Juan, Calico Jack suddenly seized a lantern and hurled that at him. Juan ducked and the missile sailed over his shoulder giving him a glancing blow before it burst into flames against the wall behind him. The grog shop proprietor, a ruddy-faced white man, at once began to beat at the flames with a broom, and when this failed, he doused them with buckets of water his serving girls rushed to him from behind the counter beneath the wash basin where the utensils and tankards were cleansed and rinsed.

Unmindful of the commotion behind them, Juan and Calico Jack fought on. Then, wearying of the sport, Juan began an aggressive course of action. He feinted several blows, then parried a vicious slash, and waded in, sending home the point of his blade between Calico Jack's ribs.

Calico Jack screamed and dropped his weapon. He fell back, staggering, and then collapsed over an upturned table, his retching mouth issuing forth blood and gore as he expired in a convulsive jerk.

There was a moment of stunned silence. Then all bedlam broke loose. The crew drew their blades and began to converge on Juan. Juan quickly stepped upon the counter and shouted at the top of his voice, 'Look behind you.'

All those advancing on him stopped in their tracks and turned. When they saw Gideon and the crew of the *Panther* drawing on them, aiming pistols and muskets, the men at once let fall their weapons. One man stepped toward Panther John and presented his sword, hilt first, 'I am Simon, Panther John. I was Calico Jack's first mate. On behalf of the crew I tender our surrender terms. Let us go and we will promise to leave you in peace and brotherhood like the old days – when Lafitte was our leader.'

Juan looked toward Gideon and his crew. All had heard. Then Juan cried out, 'What say you, men? Do we release these blackguards or do we cut them down where they stand?'

'Cut 'em down!' one man shouted.

Another waved his blade in the air and took several menacing steps toward two men he was confronting. 'I say slit their scurvy throats and be done with the lot of 'em! Wasn't they trying to do us in?'

'Hear, hear.'

Gideon stepped forward, arms lifted to get the crew's attention. When all fell silent, he said, 'Men, let us take a vote on it. All those in favor of scuttling Calico Jack's crew, say Aye.'

Half of those assembled began waving their weapons in the air and shouting, 'Aye, Aye!'

'Those opposed?'

A timid show of hands responded. Juan, standing on the table, counted. When the count was finished he looked down at Gideon. 'The crew's split.'

Gideon stood up on a chair and shouted, 'Since we're divided, men, there's only one thing to do. Let's strip 'em of their valuables and gold and put 'em permanently ashore.'

With that, the men attacked the crew in force. Not a shot was fired as Panther John's men moved against their adversaries with ferocity and anger, disarming them, then herding them against the walls to search them for their gold. When all hands present not with the *Panther*'s crew had been disarmed and divested of their valuables, Gideon and the crew went on a rampage, smashing chairs against skulls, overturning tables, and jumping over the counters to break open the kegs of rum and ale.

The grog shop proprietor came rushing to Panther John begging him to call off his men. Juan listened for several minutes and smiled down at the man, saying, 'If I do call off my men, what will you do for me?'

The proprietor rubbed his hands together anxiously, gazing up at Juan. He followed Juan's gaze across the room to the blonde serving girl who was trying to hide behind several empty barrels with the other serving girls. 'You would like sleep with Gretly?'

'Gretly is her name?' Juan said, his gaze fixed on her hungrily.

'Ja, ja,' the proprietor said.

Juan nodded. He sheathed his cutlass, put his fists on his hips and shouted for the men to belay. At once the crew responded to his command. The smashing of furniture and crockery ceased. The hands withdrew, glancing in disappointment toward Panther John.

'All right, see to our business. Gideon, take half the company aboard Calico Jack's ship and see if there's anything worthy of taking. Bring his instruments and sea chests to my cabin aboard the *Panther*. The rest of you blighters, see to it that these men are scattered down the beach. Then get on with the business of unloading our cargo. Report back here when the job's finished.'

When the men had departed, Juan smiled at the blonde serving girl and beckoned to her. She came over, her blue eyes anxiously searching Juan's face.

'Did your master tell you to sleep with me?'

The girl shyly touched a finger to her lips and bowed her head. She nodded and then after shifting her feet nervously, smiled up at him. 'Yes, he told me.'

'Do you want to sleep with me?'

'Yes.'

'Why? I am a black man.'

'You are a man – a good man,' she said. 'Those others, they are not good men. They are murderers and worse – '

'Then you don't care if I'm black and you're white?'

The girl met his questioning gaze without blinking. 'No. I see you as a man, not as a white or black one. I've heard many good things about you, Panther John. I've heard some bad things too – but those were told by your enemies – the Gaspars, and the others like Calico Jack.'

'Did it upset you to see my blade run him through?'

'It always upsets me to see men die – even dogs like Calico Jack.'

Juan smiled and took the girl by the arm. 'Shall we go up to your room?'

'As you wish, sir; but, there is one request . . .'

Juan eyed her with suspicion. He wanted to speak, to tell her that if her wish was not to go to bed with him, then he would not do so. Instead, he waited for her to continue.

'I beg you, sir,' she said, 'do not hurt me. I heard you

black men sometimes take pleasure – in hurting we white women.'

Juan closed his eyes and smiled. He snapped his head to one side in that amusing fashion of his and squinted through one eye, down his nose at her. 'Do I look like a coward who takes pleasure in hurting women?'

She shrugged and admitted she did not think so.

'Very good, then lead the way.'

Seeing the pleasant smile on his face, she chucked aside her apron and taking him by the hand, led him through the kitchen and up the puncheon steps leading to the second story of the crude building which housed the grog shop and island hostel.

They entered a large loftlike room with crown glass windows set high in dormers above their heads. The room was furnished with a large poster bed, wash stand, gilt framed mirror, and a carpet of brown animal skins.

The girl went to the windows and reached up to untie the curtains. Juan stopped her and drew her aside. 'No, I don't want you in the dark. I wish to see your body in the sunlight.'

The girl laughed. She drew away from him and tried to elude his grasp, but Juan was too fast. He caught her and drew her near, then his hands sought out the fastenings which buttoned together her tight fitting garment. The girl squirmed in his arms, but when she finally realized how determined he was, she lifted her hands to his face and clasped them over his eyes. 'You shan't look until I'm under the covers.'

Juan continued undressing her. His hands stripped away the dress and the cotton shift beneath it. Then his fingers sought out her soft curves, gently stroking and kneading until he suddenly felt something upon her body which felt strange to the touch. It seemed as though there was something on her skin, like a skin-tight sheath of leather. He pressed her away and with his hands gripping her tightly by the hips, opened his eyes.

She fought him, fought to keep him from seeing. But Juan did see. He gazed at her flesh and saw ugly burn scars marring the beauty of her hips, her breasts, the rounded curves of her legs, the soft belly.

'How did you suffer such terrible burns?'

The girl tried to conceal her scars by dropping to her

knees and doubling over, clasping her breasts to her. She began to sob and after several minutes, gazed up at him through her tears and said, 'It was Gaspar who did this to me. When I refused to be his wench, he tied me to a bed and poured hot oil on me. Then he sold me to the grog shop proprietor.'

Juan leaned toward her upraised face, took her gently by the cheeks and drew her to her feet. Then he encircled her body in his arms and held her, kissing the top of her head. After several minutes he drew her to the poster bed and laid down, pulling her on top of him, his mouth now seeking hers. When they parted after a time she asked, 'You do not mind my ugly scars? My hideous body?'

'No, I do not mind. I see you as a woman – a beautiful one with beautiful hair and beautiful eyes – blue eyes like the sea.'

The girl slipped her arms around Juan's neck and lowered her mouth to cover his. She felt his strong hands, the hands which only a short while before had so deftly killed Calico Jack, and she knew those same hands which were able to snuff out life were also able to be gentle and give life and love, even to one such as her.

NEW ORLEANS
April 17, 1834
Saturday
10 p.m.

Juan and Gideon stood against the wall of the livery stables across the broad avenue from the quay where the *Panther* was docked. They had just herded twenty-seven white girls and women into the stalls inside the barn-like structure and now they were awaiting the right moment to begin having the bound and gagged females toted catty-corner across the wet cobblestones to the ship.

Since they discovered that white women in their late teens and early twenties often fetched prices ranging from three to ten times that of house Negroes or field hands, during the past five years, Gideon, Juan, and his crew of fifteen had devoted themselves exclusively to that field of endeavor. The women they had just obtained had been kidnapped by street gangs and bands of cutthroats, at times right out of the marketplaces and right off the city streets. For the younger, more comely women, Juan paid a flat rate of five hundred per head, no questions asked. But for the older women, those between twenty-two and thirty, Juan refused to pay more than one hundred dollars a head. Women older than thirty were not bought. After the *Panther* was loaded with her clandestine cargo, they would slip away under cover of darkness, destination: the Isle of Pines and at times, when the demand was great enough, to the islands of the Caribbean.

On this Saturday night in New Orleans, Juan had a special request to fill, and so far, it looked as if he was successful. A wealthy Negro planter from Panama was at that moment sitting aboard a swift corvette which he owned, thirty miles out of New Orleans, within sight of Lafitte's old headquarters at Barrataria. The planter had promised to pay Juan and his crew ten thousand dollars a head for twenty to thirty comely young white women. He was interested only if they were French or English and if they were of fair complexion and blonde or red haired.

As usual, Juan did not question why the planter wanted so many young white girls. His only concern was the adventure of obtaining them and then smuggling them out of the port city of New Orleans, and of course, in the money too.

It mattered little to Juan that the planter had a fetish he preferred not to speak about. And it mattered less to Juan and his men that the planter had made no secret of the fact that he was a *hungan*, a witch doctor who was the leader of a sect that still practiced voodooism according to the ancient African cannibal tribal rites. So far as the crew of the *Panther* was concerned, what the planter did with the girls and women he paid so handsomely to purchase, was none of their mettle.

Pierre, emerging from the shadows near the moored ship, motioned for the waiting crew standing by to come ahead with their living bundles. One by one the men ran out of the stables, the blanketed, trussed kidnap victims slung over their shoulders like sacks of merchandize. Without incident they ran up the gangplank and deposited each female on deck where one of their fellows, standing by with a truncheon, punished them with a blow across the head or feet if they failed to remain quiet and still. When the task was done and all twenty-seven were aboard, Juan and Gideon crossed the street and boarded the ship. The plank was raised and the lines cast off as a skeleton crew aloft unfurled the main and fores'l.

Once they were at sea, Juan could relax. But as usual he did not relax for somehow nothing of late seemed to provide him with the excitement and fulfillment he had once so thoroughly enjoyed. He leaned against the rail watching the lights of New Orleans fade in the distance, thinking now about his son, Juan junior, whom he had not seen for three years ever since Maria had made him promise for the last time that he would never again set foot on Panther Cay again and never again would try to lure the boy away from her.

There was a dry, choking sensation at the back of Juan's throat when he remembered that his son's twelfth birthdate had come and gone. Each year he suffered the old anguish all over again, and as he grew older, and was now forty-three, he felt that if he had to suffer another bitter lonely year, another empty anniversary of memories, he would prefer to take his own life instead. He had long since given up trying to find someone else to fill the abyss in his own life. But now, aboard his ship, he at least felt potent and powerful and strong as ever. It was a warped sense of loyalty to the memory of days long since gone by that kept Juan constantly dwelling on the past.

He banged his fists upon the rail and turned. He clenched his teeth and cursed his foolhardiness. Why couldn't he be carefree and reckless as was Gideon and the others in his crew? Why did he always need to be so serious, so absolute an authoritarian, so unyielding a captain, so untolerant and unbending a leader?

Juan's realization struck him momentarily dumb like a thunderclap and lightning bolt that brings forth an epithany of revelations when suddenly all things become clear and all sounds become sharp as the tinkling of a silver bell; and all sights become dazzling in their clarity. He grabbed an oil lantern from beside the binnacle and walked amidship to the area where the twenty-seven women now lay trussed together, the blankets removed from over their heads, but the gags still intact in the event that some passing vessel might come to within hailing distance and by chance overhear a scream for help.

Juan passed from one woman to the next, playing the lantern light over each face, noticing the way the light illuminated their blonde and red and pale colored hair. As he walked along suddenly he saw one woman who looked so much like Maria had looked when he had first laid eyes on her thirteen years before, that he was momentarily stunned. He could not believe his eyes. He put the lantern down, knelt beside the girl, and then pushed aside some of the wide cloth which had been bound around her face to hold the gag in her mouth. He peered into her blue eyes and saw there the same frightened look he had once seen in Maria's eyes.

Suddenly, Juan was lifting the girl in his arms and carrying her bodily to his cabin. Gideon saw him and stepped aside, holding open the companionway door, grinning.

Juan swallowed hard, trying to compose himself, fighting to restrain his racing pulse, his plunging throbbing heart. He was reliving the past and the scent of this woman, the sweet feminine smell of her femininity was enough to drive him utterly mad.

He carried her into his cabin and kicked the door shut. Then he placed her upon the bunk, returned to the door and threw both bolts into place, and still without uttering a word, he returned to gaze down at her. After a long while he said, 'I want to speak to you. If I untie you and take out that gag, do you promise to be very quiet and not cry out? Blink your eyes twice if you promise.'

The girl blinked twice.

Juan drew his sheath knife and cut her free. He pulled the gag out of her mouth and helped her sit up, watching as she first touched a hand to her jaw and worked her mouth to overcome the foul taste of the rags and the stiffness, then running her white fingers through her blonde tresses. She glanced round at him and smiled, a tiny smile. 'Thank you for setting me free. Who are you?'

'Capitaine Juan Gomez, my lady.'

She smiled and frowned a little, lost in thought, trying to recall something. 'Why did your men kidnap me?'

Juan shrugged. 'That is my business.'

She laughed. Her eyes flicked as she contemplated him. 'And why are you in this business?'

'To make a lot of money.'

'Why? What can a black man do with a lot of money?'

'For one thing, he can buy and sell women like you.'

His words gave her a start. She gasped and then said, 'Oh.' She glanced around the cabin and then rested her gaze on his face again, watching as he dropped to a crouch, his eyes now level with hers. 'And what else do you plan doing with all that money?'

'Perhaps I might want to settle down and buy a plantation and raise sugar and bananas in the West Indies. I don't know really.'

'Why are you staring at me like that?'

'Something about you reminds me of someone I once knew . . .'

'You must have loved her very, very much.'

'How say you this?'

She cocked her head and then smiled. 'I can tell. Sometimes a woman instinctively senses such things.'

'Is your name – what is your name?'

She smiled. 'I am Louisa Jordain. My papa is an attorney. Your men had no right to snatch me right off the street in broad daylight in front of my door.'

Juan dipped his shoulders and made a face. 'I'm not sorry. I'm glad they kidnaped you.'

'Why?'

'So I can have you to myself.'

She stared at him, her innocent blue eyes searching his intent brown eyes. 'I – I don't understand. I'm afraid I'm not too, how shall I say – ? worldly. Yes, worldly, that's the word. I'm only eighteen, you see. I went to a convent school and I've lead a rather boring, quiet life. Never did I dream I would wake up one day and find I had been kidnaped by pirates.'

Juan felt something tighten in his chest. 'Who said I was a pirate?'

She smiled thinly. 'I know you now. I've heard more than one story about Panther John. You're Panther John, aren't you?'

Juan smiled and nodded. 'Are you frightened?'

The girl did not reply. She chewed her bottom lip. Juan recalled how Maria had also chewed her lip that day when they had quarreled, while they talked in his cabin, the very same cabin they were in now – he and this girl – this innocent young thing called Louisa Jordain.

'I asked if you were frightened.'

'Y-yes, I suppose I am.'

'Is it because I'm a black man, is that why you're afraid?'

'No, it isn't that. I'm used to gentlemen of color. We have six in our house, you know. Daddy has owned them since he was a boy.'

'Do you like these gentlemen of color who are your slaves?'

'Yes, certainly I like them. They're kind and good and they know their places.'

'Know their places? What do you mean?'

The girl wet her lips with a pink tongue. Her smooth skin had a healthy glow to it in the lantern light. It reminded him of his thoughts that night when he married Maria. Her pale white flesh had looked somewhat like the succulent flesh of a ripe peach.

'I mean, they don't get uppity or smart with you. They keep their places; whenever they pass you down the street, they step off the sidewalk to let you pass by; they know who their betters are.'

'Betters?'

The girl looked a trifle afraid at the strange expression forming in Juan's eyes. She hurriedly averted her gaze. Then she explained without facing him directly. 'Yes, they know who their betters are just as they know who their equals are.'

'I see,' Juan nodded. 'Let me see if I understand this now. What are we, you and I? Who is the better? Are you better than me?'

Without a moment's hesitation she said, 'Certainly I'm better than you. Everyone knows *that.*'

'Why?' he asked.

'Why?' she repeated. 'Don't be silly. The whole world knows that white folks are far better than ladies and gentlemen of color.'

'Am I in the same world as you?' he asked.

'Yes.'

'Then how is it *I* don't know that. Can you tell me why you – a white girl is better than I am, a black man?'

'I can't answer that.'

'Why not? If you can say it, why can't you know what you're saying?'

'Please, won't you stop this? You're confusing me.'

'You're going to be a damn sight more than just confused before this night is over.'

'I don't think I like you any more. Please release me and go away.'

Juan drew himself up to his full height. His eyes glittered as he towered above her, looking down. Through clenched teeth he said, 'Take off your clothes, white girl.'

Louisa blushed deeply. She shrank back, pressing a hand to her throat, blue eyes turned upwards in fright.

She did not argue. He reached out and seized her by the hair. She screamed. He picked up the gag which had been in her mouth and replaced it, holding her head down, forcing her jaws apart, ramming the rag into her mouth. Then he methodically began to rip off the clothes from her body. He jerked her off the bunk and half-dragged, half-carried her to the window cushions. He stood above her again, ripping every shred of clothing from her and when she was stark naked, he held her up by holding her hair at arm's length. Then he placed rough brown hands upon her soft white breasts. His mouth began to slaver as he lowered his lips to her nipples and licked first one, then the other. The girl struggled for a moment but when he shook her with such violent force that her teeth crunched, she ceased doing so.

Juan smiled and pressed her back and down upon the cushions. He arose and quickly stripped off his clothes. He then moved to her and knelt above her supple young body. He felt the breath raling in his nostrils as he bent to suckle her breasts again, and then after he had tasted of them, he kissed her on the mouth. She wrested her face away, jerking her head from side to side. Juan clamped a hold on her with one of his powerful hands and held her. He plunged his tongue deeply into her mouth and lashed her tongue with it.

Then he slid down and began to caress her hips, to knead her buttocks, to probe her secret parts with aching, hungering fingers, as his eager mouth sought the wispy down at the pit of her stomach.

Louisa whimpered and churned her hips when he found her with his tongue and his lips drew her lips inward to his. He drew deep of the heady scent of her, the soft white flawlessness of her velvety flesh and he went mad with the urgency of his searing desire.

He suckled her and plunged his tongue over her sleek wet flesh and she in response tore at his head with her fingernails and kicked at his back with the naked heels of her legs.

He wanted her to love him, not strike him. He wanted her to caress him, to want him, not to claw him and not to fight him. The churning inferno of unrequited desire ripped through Juan's veins. He felt himself reliving the past, reliving the moments he had spent in Maria's arms; but then again, *not* reliving them for Louisa was resisting, not passive as Maria had been.

Which was worse? To have a woman under him who was like a corpse? To have a woman under him who fought him?

Juan was not thinking. He had gone this way before; he had craved these same cravings before and he had lusted these same lusts before.

Suddenly he crouched above the girl, one hand clamped over her mouth, the other holding her by her writhing, struggling bared buttocks. He held his throbbing manhood against her and felt the feeble membrane yielding. The girl screamed, shrieked into the palm of his hand and her eyes widened and filled with tears. He knelt above her, one powerful brown-black arm against her weak child-woman flesh, her pale flesh, holding her imprisoned as he used her, sending himself plummeting into her again and again and again, hammering away the yielding flesh, his rough flesh, now gleaming black and livid veined, sloughed into her, then out, into her, then out. She raked his arms with her clawing fingers, but he did not feel the pain she inflicted.

Then Juan threw himself upon her with all the weight of his two hundred fifty pounds behind him. He felt her being crushed beneath his hard brown body; he felt her gasping for breath, but he did not care. He writhed and drove down into her until he felt his bones smashing into hers.

When at last he reached the summit, he fell down the heights like a fly in a vortex being sucked into a whirlpool which in turn sucked the whirlpool into another, and another.

He felt drained, but not sated. He felt hunger, but no longer desire. He remembered Maria and he remembered the son he did not know, the son he could not have, the son whose birthdays he could not attend, and he remembered most of all the terrible things Maria had said to him; the things Maria his wife had said to him during those awful moments of that day when she came to her senses with the realization she was carrying his child.

Juan looked at the girl beneath him and saw Maria and he saw all white women and he saw his wife: the woman he could not have: the woman who would not love him.

He lowered his face to her breasts but she did not stir. Yes, yes, it *was* Maria. Maria had not moved. Now this one does not move, yet she breathes.

He listened at her breast. He heard the heartbeats. He recalled having heard his unborn son's heartbeats; the heartbeats of the fetus months before birth.

Everything rolled before his eyes like a gigantic wave bursting with seaspray and froth to stifle one, to drown one. He leeched his mouth onto the naked breast of the girl and she did not stir. He sank his teeth deeper, then deeper, and finally warm blood spurted – the blood of some ancient rite recalled to memory now in the recesses of the mind. A secret rite. Cannabalistic. *Hungan* rites. Boko once described in detail. A time comes in the black man's life, the black man who is Panther John, when he got to damn eat.

Juan drank her spurting milk blood. He rolled over and held her small body aloft, her limp body above him. He bit through the flesh of the left berry-like breast and it too spurted forth life blood. He felt the gushing flow sticking upon his beard, upon his face, perhaps staining him forever, not brown, not black, but near-white like his son. The son his wife Maria is too ashamed of to ever, ever take to a town or place where other white people will see him because they will look at her, then at him and then they will know – he is a nigger.

Nigger is panther. Panther is John. John is Juan. He moaned and tore at the unconscious girl's body, the body he yearned for all his life. He threw wide her limbs and leeched his mouth against her, sinking deeply his teeth, feeling the tiny bud, slippery as a grisly gism, a mussle, muscule, oyster.

He spread wide the rounded buttocks and ripped into them. First with teeth, then with tongue, then with hands, then he ripped her flesh apart, as he had ripped and split her dress, her garments.

Juan, his head pounding, staggered to his feet. He slowly came to his senses. He gazed down at the ripped flesh, the remains he could no longer recognize. Then he calmly began to hurl the broken flesh, the torn bleeding flesh, out the window and into the seawater below.

Head pounding, almost blind from pain, Juan staggered to the locker where he kept the bottles of rum and liqueurs and wines. He brought them out, then uncorking them, poured them over his head, bathing himself in them, washing off the blood, the gore, the scent of her.

When he had emptied every bottle and every jug he could find, he calmly wiped himself dry, carefully dressed in the finest garments he could find in his sea chest, and then he returned to the brisk fresh coolness of the deck above.

Gideon, standing by the helmsman, smiled at Juan, a knowing smile. He had heard the splashings off the fantail. He knew and he understood.

They rendezvoused at Barrataria and after the girls and the money changed hands, Juan set a course for Tampa. He had received word from one of his spies that a dealer there was offering a comely lot of Spanish beauties. It had been a long while since Juan had visited Tampa. He had avoided that area like the proverbial bad luck hoodoo ever since he and Gideon and Boko had stolen Gaspar's ship and made off with it. Every single time since then he had carefully avoided making any mention of Gasparilla Island or the Tampa area, which had been Leon Gaspar's stamping grounds.

It was as if Juan Gomez had somehow known all the years

of his life that if he was to survive and live to a ripe old age, he was to avoid – at all costs – Gasparilla's old stamping grounds.

On the morning of April 19, 1834, at four a.m. on a deserted lane outside the city of Tampa, Capitaine Juan Gomez, who was also known in this life as Panther John, was set upon by men who had sworn to derive satisfaction which their leaders, Leon Gaspar, and later, Don Jose Gaspar had failed to obtain. They fell upon Juan Gomez and beat him to death with short cudgels: cudgels which they had fashioned from the thigh and forearm bones of none other than Leon and Don Gaspar themselves.

Epilogue:

In the year 1906, at Panther Key, Florida, one Juan Gomez was found dead of accidental drowning. According to those who found his body, he was supposed to be over a hundred years old and had once been known as Panther John, the pirate captain.

Today the truth is known. The Juan Gomez who drowned that day in 1906 after having tripped and snared his own legs in a fishing net, was none other than the mulatto son who was born to Juan Gomez and Maria Dunsmore Gomez on that day in April of 1822.

It is not known if Panther John's treasure chests, allegedly eight of them, have ever been dug up. However there are some who claim Juan Gomez, being a simple and content man, had no need to dig up more than one of his father's treasure chests during his lifetime.

Book Tokens

Give them the pleasure of choosing

Book Tokens can be bought and exchanged at most bookshops in Great Britain and Ireland.

NEL BESTSELLERS

T045 528	THE STAND	*Stephen King*	£1.75
T046 133	HOW GREEN WAS MY VALLEY	*Richard Llewellyn*	£1.00
T039 560	I BOUGHT A MOUNTAIN	*Thomas Firbank*	95p
T033 988	IN THE TEETH OF THE EVIDENCE	*Dorothy L. Sayers*	90p
T038 149	THE CARPETBAGGERS	*Harold Robbins*	£1.50
T041 719	HOW TO LIVE WITH A NEUROTIC DOG	*Stephen Baker*	75p
T040 925	THE PRIZE	*Irving Wallace*	£1.65
T034 755	THE CITADEL	*A.J. Cronin*	£1.10
T042 189	STRANGER IN A STRANGE LAND	*Robert Heinlein*	£1.25
T037 053	79 PARK AVENUE	*Harold Robbins*	£1.25
T042 308	DUNE	*Frank Herbert*	£1.50
T045 137	THE MOON IS A HARSH MISTRESS	*Robert Heinlein*	£1.25
T040 933	THE SEVEN MINUTES	*Irving Wallace*	£1.50
T038 130	THE INHERITORS	*Harold Robbins*	£1.25
T035 689	RICH MAN, POOR MAN	*Irwin Shaw*	£1.50
T043 991	EDGE 34: A RIDE IN THE SUN	*George G. Gilman*	75p
T037 541	DEVIL'S GUARD	*Robert Elford*	£1.25
T042 774	THE RATS	*James Herbert*	80p
T042 340	CARRIE	*Stephen King*	80p
T042 782	THE FOG	*James Herbert*	90p
T033 740	THE MIXED BLESSING	*Helen Van Slyke*	£1.25
T038 629	THIN AIR	*Simpson & Burger*	95p
T038 602	THE APOCALYPSE	*Jeffrey Konvitz*	95p
T046 850	WEB OF EVERYWHERE	*John Brunner*	85p

NEL P.O. BOX 11, FALMOUTH TR10 9EN, CORNWALL

Postage charge:
U.K. Customers. Please allow 30p for the first book plus 15p per copy for each additional book ordered to a maximum charge of £1.29 to cover the cost of postage and packing, in addition to cover price.

B.F.P.O. & Eire. Please allow 30p for the first book plus 15p per copy for the next 8 books, thereafter 6p per book, in addition to cover price.

Overseas Customers. Please allow 50p for the first book plus 15p per copy for each additional book, in addition to cover price.

Please send cheque or postal order (no currency).

Name..

Address...

....

Title...

While every effort is made to keep prices steady, it is sometimes necessary to increase prices at short notice. New English Library reserve the right to show on covers and charge new retail prices which may differ from those advertised in the text or elsewhere. (3)